THE FICTIONAL NEMESIS

By Greg Fowlkes

Includes a Bonus Story from the book

A FICTIONAL DETECTIVE TRIFECTA:

THE FICTIONAL DETECTIVE SPEAKS WITH THE DEAD

and a Sneak Preview from the book

The Uncorrupted Corpse

THE FICTIONAL NEMESIS

© 2017 The Fictional Press
www.TheFictionalPress.com

Published by Intrepid Ink, LLC

Intrepid Ink, LLC provides full publishing services to authors of fiction and non-fiction books, eBooks and websites. From editing to formatting, to publishing, to marketing, Intrepid Ink gets your creative works into the hands of the people who want to read them.

Find out more at www.IntrepidInk.com.

ISBN 13: 978-1-943403-45-5

Printed in the United States of America

Books by Greg Fowlkes

From the Wizard at Law Series:
The Laws of Magic
Trial by Magic

From the Murder on Mars Series:
Blood Red Sands of Mars
A Death at Station Alpha
A Corpse in Hut Town
Murder at the Mars Club

From the Fictional Detective Series:
The Fictional Detective
A Fictional Detective Trifecta

Star City Stories: Space Opera Noir Featuring Frank Sladek

The Uncorrupted Corpse

Tequila Visions

Cargo From Paradise

Ice Viking

ABOUT THE AUTHOR

A Wisconsin native, Greg Fowlkes received his master's degree in physics from the University of Wisconsin. Since graduation, he has had a career developing telecommunications software. A lifelong reader of science fiction and fantasy, he began writing while still in graduate school, though it would be several decades until his first work, *The Fictional Detective*, was published. This was soon followed by the collection of novellas, *The Laws of Magic*, and the novel *The Blood Red Sands of Mars*. His work explores the conjunction of science fiction, fantasy, and the hard-boiled detective stories. His series includes the Murder on Mars novels, which focus on a law enforcement team on a Martian colony in the not-too-distant future; the *Wizard at Law* stories, which deal with a lawyer with an unusual set of clients; and *The Fictional Detective* stories and novel about a hard-boiled detective with existential issues. His latest series, the *Star City Stories*, features a private detective whose beat is a hollowed out asteroid orbiting a brown dwarf, and takes place some thousand years in the future. He was also published a more or less conventional detective novel, *The Uncorrupted Corpse*.

In his spare time, what there is of it, Greg Fowlkes plays guitar and mandolin, makes furniture, and takes his two Shiba Inus, Toshiro and Yojimbo, for long walks.

Prologue

I was going through Ezekial Handler's things the other day. It was late November, that time of year the only purpose of which is to keep Thanksgiving and Christmas apart. The weather was cold and rainy which had discouraged me from walking down to the corner bar and drinking beer while staring at the bottles lining the wall behind the bar. Instead, I was poking through Handler's stuff looking for ideas, but mostly just wasting time, an occupation I've found I'm pretty good at.

Handler had been a writer, a relatively famous one. I'm a writer now, too, or at least I'm trying to be one. I used to be a private detective, but I'd given that up after my last case, which had been investigating Handler's death. There hadn't seemed to be much of a future in being a private dick, or much of a past, either, for that matter, at least for me. I've kept the office, though. Before that—well, sometimes I'm not even sure that there was a before that, at least for me.

I had some time on my hands because I'd sent off the final proofs for *Death Buys a Condo*, and my publisher hadn't gotten back to me about a proposal for my next book. She'd asked for something a little more hard-boiled, so I'd sent in an outline for something that I was tentatively titling *Bloody Mary, Mob Hit-Woman*. I wasn't sure if that was the kind of thing that she had in mind, but then I was still new to the writing game.

Like many writers, Ezekial O. Handler had been something of a pack rat. He'd kept all the old manuscripts and notes for each of his books, numerous notebooks full of ideas for future stories, and others detailing clever ways of knocking someone off including ways to avoid detection or get caught. He'd even kept folders full of rejection slips, though those mostly dated from the early days before he'd become a best-selling author of detective fiction. When his mansion had been cleared out after his death, all this literary detritus had been shoved into a dozen or so banker's boxes which now sat in a corner of my office gathering dust. The reason that those boxes were in my office was that in his will, Handler had named his mistress as the heir to his literary estate. Janet, my wife, had been his mistress. Of course, we didn't meet until after Handler was dead. That's how we met, when Janet had walked into my office, this office, to ask me to find Handler's killer.

After we were married, Janet had suggested that I give up the private investigation business and try my hand at writing detective fiction. We certainly didn't need the little money I was bringing in as a P.I., and when Janet makes a suggestion, I tend to listen. She had, after all, saved my life with a well-aimed slug from a .45 automatic. But that's another story.

I'd just finished thumbing through the notebook Handler had kept for *The Uncorrupted Corpse*, the last book he'd had published before he'd been murdered. I'd read the book, it was pretty grim stuff. It was when I was putting the notebook back in the box that I had found it, buried at the bottom of the pile.

"It", was a bound volume, kind of like the ones teenage girls use as diaries, except larger. It even had one of those locking clasps to keep out the prying eyes of anyone not equipped with a paper clip; only somehow this lock seemed a little more serious. At the time, I'd thought it odd, because most of the notebooks Handler had used were of the ordinary spiral bound variety, the kind that school kids use and which you can pick up at any drug or stationary store. This volume, though, had obviously been specially made. It was covered in a dark leather from the hide of an animal I couldn't identify. It had to have been quite expensive.

It was pretty obvious that whatever Handler had written within had been something that he had wanted to keep private. I wasn't sure that I wanted to find out what was inside. Towards the last, Handler had become interested in what, for want of a better term, could be called the "black arts." He'd acquired a bunch of old books on magic and sorcery, not the kind of thing that you can pick up in ordinary book stores, but the real deal; grimoires and spell books hundreds of years old and written in Latin, Hebrew, and other, more obscure, languages. He'd seemed to have had some premonition of the events leading up to his murder and had taken steps to insure that his murderer was brought to justice. Which is where I came into the picture.

Though I'd never met him while alive, he had arranged for a series of, for want of a better term, "communications" to fall into my hands, communications that seemed to predict my actions and which eventually were to lead me to his killer. The most disturbing aspect of this was not the fact that he had been influencing my actions, but the implication that I was not just being manipulated, but that I had somehow been *created* to avenge his death. Coupled with that implication was the fact that my own recollections of my past are vague at best. To this day I can't prove that everything Handler claimed wasn't true.

I'd nearly gotten myself killed confronting Handler's murderer, which had left me in a somewhat fragile state. Having my very existence called into question had driven me into a funk that ended in a week long drinking binge. It had taken Janet to pull me out of it.

I had a sense that reading Handler's darkest thoughts might reopen old wounds. Life had turned out pretty good for me. I had money, a blossoming career as a writer, a dream wife; in short, all that a man could ask for. Did I want to risk that?

I took the diary or journal or whatever you want to call it and put it in the back of the bottom drawer of the filing cabinet that stood against the wall. Then I locked the drawer, and put the key inside the safe I had in the office. I vowed never to open it again.

Chapter One

I'd gotten a call from Flannigan asking me to meet him at the Preston Arms. Flannigan was a police lieutenant with eighteen years on the force. He was a friend of mine, though not what you'd call close. More the let's go have a beer or watch a game type. Still, he'd been best man at my wedding, which must count for something.

On the phone Flannigan had sounded worried which was unusual for him. We'd been to a basketball game the night before, and it hadn't seemed like there had been anything on his mind. During the time he'd been a cop he'd seen just about everything, so it would take a lot to rattle him, but he had sounded rattled when he called.

The Preston Arms is a high-rise building of luxury apartments and condominiums in the heart of the downtown shopping district. Rents are high, but the amenities make it worth it for those who can afford them. I knew a few of the people who lived in the building, mostly through Janet, and had been in it several times before.

Of course, there hadn't been a brace of squad cars parked out in front with their lights flashing on those occasions. The meat wagon from the M.E.'s office was there as well, which gave me a good idea of what was going on. What I couldn't figure out was why Flannigan had called me in. I'd quit the P.I. racket for good, and the crimes that I dealt with these days are all of the fictional variety.

There was a uniformed patrolman standing guard at the entrance who asked me my business. He was polite about it, but firm, implying that I'd better have a good reason for being there if I wanted to get inside. I gave him my name. Flannigan had obviously left word because after giving me the once over with his eyes, the cop opened the door and said I should go on up to apartment 811. For some reason the number sounded familiar, but I couldn't recall why.

I rode the elevator up to the eighth floor. When I stepped out into the hallway there was another cop waiting. Word must have passed up somehow, because he didn't bother asking who I was. Maybe he just figured that if I'd made it that far I must be okay. He didn't need to give me directions, either. It was pretty clear which apartment was 811. The door was open, and there was a fingerprint man dusting the knob. He looked up as I approached, but then went back about his business.

There was a sense of *déjà vu* as I walked through the door. It came to me why the apartment number had seemed familiar. The apartment belonged to a colleague of mine, and Janet and I had gone to a release party there about six months earlier. I was beginning to get an idea of why Flannigan had asked me to come down, and I wasn't liking what I'd come up with.

It had been a while since I'd been at a real crime scene. They can seem pretty chaotic. There was a whole crew of crime lab technicians taking photos and dusting various objects for prints. There were a couple of guys from the M.E.'s office waiting with an empty gurney to take the corpse away. It was pretty obvious from all the activity that there was going to be a corpse. They don't normally lay on that much of an effort for a simple B. & E.

From my previous visit, I had a general idea of the layout of the apartment. The entryway opened out into a large living room, the far end of which was a wall of glass providing a great view of the city and the lake beyond. The dining room and a small kitchen were off to the left while to the right there was the master bedroom and another room that the owner had used as a study. The action appeared to be centered in the study, so I poked my head in through the door.

One wall was taken up with floor to ceiling bookcases in dark mahogany. In the corner was an overstuffed arm chair in red leather flanked by a reading lamp and side table. In the middle of the room was a large desk with a typewriter, a phone and an answering machine. That's where the corpse was, sitting in a chair in front of the desk.

There wasn't much doubt as to cause of death, the back of the head had been smashed and blood and brains were dripping onto the thick pile of the white carpet. There wasn't any doubt as to the identity of the victim, either. It was Joshua Black, or at least that was the name under which he published his detective stories. I think his real name had been something like Sam Blackman, but he'd become so well known as an author that no one ever used that anymore.

Flannigan was standing next to the desk, pushing papers around using a pen so as not to leave any fingerprints. As I entered the room, he looked up, a sad and confused expression on his face.

Like a good cop, Flannigan got right to the point. "The victim had a maid service that comes in to clean up every morning. It was the maid that discovered the body this morning. The M.E. thinks that he was killed last night. He estimates about 8:00 P.M. give or take a few hours. We know that Black had dinner at 6:00 P.M. at a restaurant just down the street, Giovanni's. There is a call on the answering machine at 9:15. Black didn't answer it. Of course, he might still have been alive, but it does kind of point to Black being killed sometime between say 7:30 and 9:15 P.M."

"That sounds reasonable," I responded. I wasn't sure why Flannigan was making such a big deal about the time.

It didn't seem to make much difference one way or the other, at least to me.

"I believe you knew the victim, Frank?"

"Yeah, we'd met a few times, professionally, that is. He'd invited Janet and I to a party he held when his last book came out. That was about six months ago. I don't remember exactly when, but I can call Janet and get the date for you if it's important."

"I don't know. It may be. But you were competitors?"

"I wouldn't exactly put it that way. We both wrote detective stories, but it's not like we were in the same league. Black had a couple of dozen books to his credit, half of which made the best-seller list. My second book is just going to press. Black knew Janet through her association with Handler. He was kind enough to give me some advice and introduce me to some of the other writers in town. I knew him, but it's not like we were close or anything. We certainly weren't rivals. What's this all about, anyway?"

"Do you have a twin I don't know about, Frank?" It was a strange question for Flannigan to ask. He knows my recollections of my past are pretty sketchy. There's not much on record, either.

"I'm not sure I like where you're going with these questions, Flannigan."

In response, Flannigan said, "There's something that you've got to see, Frank."

"What?"

"It's not here. Come with me." He was sounding more like the cop that he was than the friend I'd thought him.

Flannigan led me back through the living-room and out into the hallway. We got into the elevator and he punched the button for the basement. He did all this without saying a word. The basement of the Preston Arms isn't quite as luxurious as the upstairs, but it's nice enough. It was certainly clean. We walked down a hall past the laundry facilities to a door labeled "Security." There was another sign that ominously declared "Authorized Personnel Only." Flannigan knocked and a large black man in a very neat blue blazer and highly polished black shoes stuck his head out. He looked as if he'd played defensive end at one time. There was an embroidered patch on the blazer that read "Preston Arms" and "Security." If I had lived in the building he certainly would have made me feel secure.

"Lt. Flannigan. What can I do for you?" The voice was polished and deep.

"I'd like you to run the video for Mr. Slade."

"Of course. This way."

The office wasn't large, but it was comfortable. There was a desk, a comfortable looking chair, and a wall of CCTV monitors, showing the lobby door, the elevator, and the garage entrance. The images were all in black and white, but remarkably clear. The management had clearly not skimped on equipment.

The security man must have had the tape cued up, because all he had to do was press a button on the video recorder and another of the monitors came to life. This one showed a man entering the lobby. There was a date code running at the bottom of the screen. It read "20:00 12/14," which was the evening before. The man looked familiar. There was a good reason for that. It was me.

"Can you explain this, Frank?"

"You can't believe that's me, Flannigan, can you? I wasn't here last night. I've got an alibi—"

"I know—"

The reason Flannigan knew I had an alibi was because he was it. I'd been given a couple of tickets to the basketball game the night before. Janet isn't a big fan, so I'd asked Flannigan. We'd had a couple of beers and some burgers beforehand, gone to the game, and stopped for another beer afterwards. The game had started at 7:30 and run until a little before ten. At 8:00 P.M. we'd both been in sitting in the stands watching the game.

Chapter Two

Flannigan was silent as we rode the elevator back up to Black's apartment. I couldn't say that I blamed him; I didn't have much to say myself. What the security video had shown was clearly impossible. The recording had been clear, the lighting good. The figure seen entering the lobby hadn't just looked like me, it had been me. Yet, at that same instant of time, I had been nearly two miles away watching a basketball game, a fact for which I had an impeccable witness, Flannigan himself.

While we had been down in the security office, Black's body had been loaded onto the gurney, and the M.E. crew was getting ready to transport it to the morgue. It looked like the crime scene technicians were about to wrap up their work as well. Every inch of the apartment had been photographed, all of the relevant surfaces had been dusted for fingerprints, and a big swatch of the carpet containing the blood and brains of Black had been removed and placed in a plastic bag. The latter was probably just as well, I doubted that the carpet could ever have been cleaned, and even if it could, would the next tenant want it?

The chief technician came over and announced, "We're pretty much done here, lieutenant."

"Good. Any idea about the murder weapon?"

"I'm pretty sure that it was this baby." He held up an evidence bag with a metal statuette. It was an award that Black had gotten for one of his books. Blood covered one corner of the base.

"Any fingerprints?"

"A couple of good ones. Left hand, thumb and middle finger. Pretty clear. Shouldn't have much problem matching them if you find the killer."

Flannigan looked at me. I could guess what he was thinking. Would the prints match the ones on my hand? After the technician had left he commented, "I don't suppose you remember picking up that statue when you were at the party here?"

"That was six months ago. I can't say that I didn't, but even if I had, Black had a maid service. I'm sure that it would have been wiped clean since then."

"Yeah," he responded, shaking his head. "Let's get out of here, Frank. I could use a drink."

"Aren't you on duty?"

"Does it matter?"

"Not to me."

I could tell Flannigan was bothered by this business, and I thought I knew why. He's got some of the same problems with his past that I do. I'm pretty sure that he is one of the "others" that Handler had mentioned in his last letter to me, the one that arrived after Janet had killed his killer. Whether Flannigan had any sense of that, I didn't know. We've never talked about it, and I've never shown him the letter.

One good thing about this town is that you never have to go far to find a bar. It turns out there was one just around the corner from the Preston. It was still early, about eleven o'clock, and the place was empty except for the bartender and a waitress getting ready for the lunch crowd. We positioned ourselves at the end of the bar and ordered a couple of beers. I was kind of relieved that Flannigan hadn't ordered anything stronger, because it looked as though he was tempted.

After we got our beers he waited until the bartender had moved away before asking, "Okay, Frank. What the hell is going on?"

"What do you mean? You can't think I had anything to do with Black's death? You were sitting right next to me during the whole game. The only time I got up was during halftime to go to the bathroom, and even then, I was out of the seat for only a few minutes. Certainly not enough time to get from the arena to Black's apartment and back."

"I know that, Frank. But I also know that the guy in the video was you, too. If you hadn't been right next to me at the time, I would be prepared to swear to that in court. I can't figure who, what, why, or where, but something is going on. I may not understand it, but I can feel something isn't right."

"You'll have to do better than that, Flannigan. What's really eating at you?"

The police lieutenant took a long swig of his beer and spent a moment staring at the backbar.

"This is going to sound crazy, Frank—"

"Not any crazier than me showing up in that video."

"I've had this feeling. I've had it for some time. Since the Handler case. I've felt that I'm not like most other people. That there's something different about me."

"Lots of cops feel that way, Flannigan. It comes with the territory."

"That's not what I'm talking about, and you know it, Frank. You know it because you feel it too."

"What do you mean, exactly?" I tried not to show it, but I was interested in what Flannigan had to say, very interested.

"I can't remember things, things about my past. Everything before the Handler case is just kind of fuzzy. Oh, I know things, like the fact that I've been on the force for nearly twenty years, that I went to school, did a hitch in the army, all the normal things you'd expect. It's just that I don't remember them. Can you understand that? I know things but I don't remember them. It's like they happened to someone else." There was a tone in Flannigan's voice that in anyone else I'd say was verging on hysteria. "But, of course you understand, because you're like that too, aren't you?"

Flannigan was getting too close to my biggest fear, closer than I wanted. I wasn't sure how he'd reached this point. As far as I knew, Handler had never contacted him about the business. But Flannigan wasn't stupid either, despite his big Irish cop exterior.

"I'm not sure I follow you, Flannigan."

"Oh, I think you do, Frank. For a long time, I thought everyone was like us, that for everyone the past was just a hazy blur of things that you know you should know, but don't. But it's not like that for most people, is it, Frank? Most people can remember who their fifth grade teacher was, they can remember the first girl they kissed, the dog they had when they were a kid, because all those experiences are real, they are things that actually happened to them. But for a few people it's different, people like you, like me, like Janet, like that singer, LaTouche, at the Blue Angel. For us the past is like—is like a description of a character in one of those detective books Handler wrote, you know, where a character's whole life and personality is summed up in one paragraph. Tell me I'm wrong, Frank. Tell me I'm crazy."

Flannigan's voice had been rising and the bartender was giving us a questioning look.

"Settle down, Flannigan. You'll have the bartender calling the cops. Let's say you're right. That you are different. That I'm different, too. Just what are you implying?"

"I don't know, Frank. And that's what has me worried."

I didn't doubt Flannigan. I'd thought that I'd come to terms with what I was or wasn't, that my own doubts were behind me. But they weren't.

"I'm going to tell you something, Flannigan. I haven't told anyone else, not even Janet. Especially not Janet. You've got to promise me you won't tell anyone else. If you do, they'll think I'm crazy and they'll probably think you are, too."

"I promise, Frank."

I took a long swig of beer, preparing what I was going to say, knowing that it was going to sound nuts, but knowing as well that it was the truth.

"It goes back to the Handler case. All through the case I kept coming across things that Handler had written, a couple of typewritten paragraphs here, a few hand written sentences there, all describing in exact detail things that had happened recently, things that had happened after Handler was murdered, and each one was another step on the way towards solving the crime, to finding out who killed Ezekial O. Handler. Now there are only two ways that I can see that Handler could have written those things. One is if he was some sort of prescient, that he could see the future."

"Do you really believe that?"

"I didn't say I did. I said that there were two ways Handler could have written those things. That was one; the other was if Handler was somehow causing things to come out a certain way."

"That's crazy, Frank."

"Isn't it, though?"

"You can't really believe that Handler could influence people's actions even after he was dead?"

"After I'd cleared up the case and Buckley was dead, I received an envelope from Handler's lawyer. Inside was a check for ten grand and an envelope containing a letter that was dated the day he was killed. I've never mentioned this to Janet, Flannigan, and you'll understand why.

"The letter was an apology and an explanation of sorts. In it, Handler claimed that he had been messing around with magic, not parlor tricks, but real, honest-to-god sorcery. He'd discovered that he was going to be killed, I'm not quite sure how. For some reason, he couldn't stop his murder from happening, but he could take steps to insure that his killer was brought to justice. That's where you and I come in.

"Handler had always had a gift with creating detailed, believable characters in his books. Well, his experiments in sorcery had given him a way to create flesh and blood characters. He'd started out small, at first. Armand O'Hara, the ex-jockey who owns the newsstand in the building where I have my office was his first attempt. His proof of concept, if you will. I'm not sure, but I think Josephine LaTouche came next, then you, then Janet. With each attempt, he got better. Finally, there was me. The little scraps of plot that he left for me to find were his way of guiding me in my quest. They worked. In the end, I was able to discover that his publisher, Buckley, had murdered him because Handler was going to jump to another publisher. I confronted Buckley, and—well you know the rest."

I'd wound myself up pretty good in the telling of the tale. Flannigan just sat there for a moment, his mouth hanging open. Then he began to laugh, loud enough that the bartender gave us another dirty look.

"You really had me going there for a minute, Frank. That's quite a story, but then I forget, you're a professional author now, aren't you?"

"It's not a story, Flannigan. I can show you Handler's letter and all the things he wrote."

"You don't actually believe that hooey, do you?"

"Look. Handler was going a little crazy there at the end. All that magic business was affecting him. Just read *The Uncorrupted Corpse.* It's quite dark and pretty ambiguous at the end. It wouldn't have taken a genius to realize that Buckley might try to kill him. After all, I figured it out. And as for the bits of plot that he left for me to find—well, he knew the people involved, he was good at reading people, it's not that big a leap to think that he could predict our actions well enough to write them down before the fact, particularly as the revelations were steering things in the direction he wanted them to go. There doesn't have to be anything mystical or metaphysical involved."

"Is that the way you think, Frank?"

"That's the way I want to think, Flannigan. Don't you?"

"But what about the memory thing? How do you explain that?"

"I don't. But how do we really know that everyone else's memories are as sharp as they claim they are? How can anyone *really* know what's going on inside somebody else's skull?"

"Okay, Frank. Say what you've just told me is true, that Handler was nuts and it was all just a big mind game that he was playing, how does any of that explain how someone that looked just like you walked into the Preston Arms and bashed in Joshua Black's skull?"

I took another long pull on my beer and set the empty glass down on the bar.

"It doesn't, Flannigan, and that's what worries me."

Chapter Three

I've never quite figured out how a low-rent private dick like me ended up with the wife I did. Janet is the kind of woman you really only find between the covers of a book, the kind that Handler and Black wrote. She's a tall, slender blonde with curves in all the right places. She's smart, educated, and classy, besides. Add to that the fact that she's a darn good cook and—well you get the idea. She's also a dead shot with a .45 automatic, something to which I owe my continued existence.

Janet had been Handler's mistress, and we'd met when she hired me to find out who had been responsible for the writer's death. At the time, the police had been treating the case as an automobile accident. After the case—well, I'd gone on a weeklong bender. It had been Janet that had pulled me out of it. After a while, we got married, and I moved into the apartment Handler had set her up with.

After my drink with Flannigan, I'd had to go down to the station to make a statement. It was nearly five when I got home. I opened the apartment door to the smell of a roasting chicken. It smelled wonderful, but I wasn't sure that I was in the mood for dinner.

Janet must have read my mood from the expression on my face.

"Frank, what's wrong? You look like the world is collapsing around you."

"Josh Black is dead. He was murdered in his apartment. Flannigan asked me to meet him at the crime scene."

"Whatever for? He knows you're not a private investigator anymore."

"He had some questions because I knew Black and had been to his apartment a few times."

Janet thought this over for a moment. She was standing in the doorway of the kitchen looking the model of a housewife with an apron over a pair of trim black slacks and a red sweater. There was a large spoon in her right hand.

"What aren't you telling me, Frank?"

Janet always seems to know what I'm thinking, almost as if she were reading a few pages ahead in the book of our lives.

"There was a surveillance camera in the lobby of Black's building. The tape from that camera has a picture of a man the police think might be the killer. The thing is, the man in the image was me."

Now some women, when confronted with a statement like that, might go to pieces, either that, or start in wondering what their husband has been up to. Not Janet. She tends to view things like that coolly and dispassionately, like when she shot Buckley between the eyes.

"When did this happen?" she asked.

"Last night, around eight."

"But you were at a basketball game with—"

"—yeah, I was at the game with Flannigan. I couldn't ask for a much better alibi than that, could I? Still, I'm not happy with the idea that someone is running around with my face committing murder."

"So, this man looked a lot like you. The police can't actually think that you had anything to do with it. Especially if you were with Lt. Flannigan at the time the crime was committed."

"He didn't just resemble me, Janet. He *was* me. He would have fooled Flannigan if I hadn't been sitting courtside with him. Hell, it would have fooled me if I didn't know better. As it is, Flannigan is in a tizzy wondering what the hell is going on."

"But they can't possibly think you had anything to do with Joshua's death, can they? After all you're alibi—"

"—my alibi is water tight. No, I'm off the hook so far. But that still doesn't explain who this guy who looks like me is. Flannigan actually asked me if I had a long lost twin. What could I say? You know that my memories of my childhood are pretty sketchy. Maybe I do have a murderous twin brother. I can't rule it out." Listening to myself, I knew I was working myself up to the same kind of state that Flannigan was in.

Janet sensed that and reacted in a practical manner.

"Look, Frank. Dinner will be ready in half an hour. Why don't you pour yourself a drink, open the wine, and relax until then. We can talk about things after dinner."

One of the things that I like about my wife is that she always takes things in stride, always knows how to defuse situations. I took her advice and poured a couple of inches of Scotch into a glass, and then added a couple of ice cubes for good measure. Janet went back into the kitchen from where I could hear cooking noises. I took a sip of the drink and then fumbled around with the cork of the bottle of wine she'd set out on the table. After pouring some of the wine to let it breathe, I went into the living room. I didn't feel like sitting, so I just stood staring out the window at the lights of the city.

Dinner passed quietly, with both of us avoiding the subject of Black's death. It was a good dinner, roasted chicken, wild rice, and Brussels sprouts, but I don't remember tasting much of it. Janet tried to keep my mind off things by asking questions about my next book. I could tell that she wasn't that thrilled with the concept, but she made some good suggestions, anyway.

After we'd finished and were sitting around the table drinking coffee she said, "This business is still bothering you, isn't it, Frank?"

"Yeah. I admit, I don't know what's going on. I have a feeling that there's more to it than just some guy who happens to look like me."

As I said that, I looked up at Janet. There was a tenseness about her that was so unlike her normal self. I'd never told her about the contents of Handler's last letter, the one where he claimed that I, along with a number of other people, were all his creation, and that Janet was among those that he had created. It had seemed such a crackpot idea at the time that it hadn't seemed worth mentioning. Later, when I had tried to check up on him by investigating my own past—well, then I wasn't so sure, but it wasn't something that I had wanted to burden her with. I think, though, that she had her own suspicions that things weren't what they seemed.

"Maybe you should consult someone professional, Frank."

"Are you talking about a psychiatrist? Do you really think I need to talk to a shrink?" I wasn't particularly comfortable with the idea. I was too afraid of what might turn up. There had been times in the past when my psyche had been teetering on the edge. I didn't want to do anything to push it over. I had too much to lose.

"No, that wasn't what I was thinking of, Frank. I don't think that you are any crazier than I am. What I was thinking was that if the killer is using some sort of illusion to impersonate you, maybe you should talk to an expert in that field. Someone like the Professor."

Professor Longwell wasn't really a professor, and, as far as I knew, Longwell was just a stage name. He was the last of a dying breed, an old time carney and sometime con-man who had switched to stage magic when the carnivals had died off. As an illusionist, he was probably third-rate at best, but he'd been around a long time and knew all the tricks and lore of the trade. He also seemed to be an actual medium that occasionally was able to contact the spirit world, though that wasn't a fact he generally advertised. He, of all the persons not touched by Handler, seemed to have some inkling that there was something different about me.

"That's not a bad idea, Janet. He might have some idea of how to pull something like this off. I should have thought of that myself."

"Which just goes to show, I'm good for something," Janet quipped.

"Oh, I can think of a number of things you're good for."

Chapter Four

As usual, my wife's advice was sound. If there was anyone I knew who might be able to make sense out of the situation, it was the Professor. Fortunately, it was a Thursday, and the Professor had a long standing engagement at the Blue Angel to perform on Tuesdays and Thursdays. I offered to take Janet along, but she declined. The Blue Angel isn't her sort of place.

I can't say that it's my sort of place, either. The Blue Angel is a dive nightclub with Bohemian pretensions. The décor is sort of a cross between a high school production of the musical *Cabaret* and a set design for a film school remake of the Marlene Dietrich film by the same name. Most of the entertainment consists of female impersonators with varying degrees of talent interspersed with a few off-color comedians. The audience tends to what Janet would call the eclectic. I'd call most of them just odd. The Blue Angel has also become fashionable amongst those looking for a safe venture into the wild side, though I don't know how many of those are repeat customers.

I'd stumbled onto the Blue Angel while looking for clues in the Handler case. Handler had been friends with the headliner, a torch singer who used the stage name Josephine LaTouche, though he/she had formerly been a steelworker named Joseph Jaworski. As far as I know, the relationship between Handler and LaTouche had been platonic at best. Considering that Janet had been Handler's idea of mistress, I didn't have any doubts about which way the late author had swung. I'd suspected at the time that the friendship Handler had had with the singer was because she/he seemed like he/she could be a character from one of his books. Later, I came to suspect that she *was* a character from one of his books.

The Professor I had come to know somewhat later. He'd been the medium at a séance I'd attended. I'd been hired by the wife of a man that had been murdered, and the wife had insisted that her husband had information for me. The Professor had gone into a trance and acted as spiritual intermediary. I don't really believe in that sort of thing, but the information panned out and led me to the murderer. I know most mediums are bogus. Even the Professor admits that. Maybe it was all a con on his part, though what he got out of it in that case, I can't imagine. The Professors claims that he never remembers what goes on in a trance. I have no reason to doubt him.

I'm not a regular at the Blue Angel, but I'm well enough known that the bouncer at the door let me in without collecting a cover. I paused at the top of the stairs for a moment to adjust to the weather. The lighting was dim and I have a sneaking suspicion that the management runs a fog machine just in case the patrons don't provide enough smoke on their own for the correct atmosphere. The dim lighting also helps to hide the peeling paint on the ceiling.

I moved on over to the bar where the bartender nodded in recognition.

"Is the Professor around yet?"

"Yeah, he's backstage in his dressing room."

"Okay if I go on back?"

"It's fine by me, man," the bartender responded with a shrug.

I was familiar enough with the layout of the place that I managed to make my way to the door leading to the back without bumping into any of the tables. Not that it would have mattered much. It was early yet and the crowd was pretty sparse, a few college kids clustered around one of the front tables, an ambiguous couple at one in the back, and a well-dressed party of four talking a little too loudly to be completely sober.

Backstage, all the pretense was gone. The lighting was brighter than out front, but only just enough to reveal the dirt and the cracked plaster. I found the Professor's dressing room by looking for the door with a cardboard sign that read "Professor Longwell." I noticed it didn't have a star on it. I knocked.

The Professor replied "Enter," in a somewhat theatrical voice.

The dressing room was about six feet wide and maybe sixteen feet long. Half of the space was taken up with costumes and various magic gizmos used in the act, including a cage with a pair of white rabbits munching on lettuce. At the far end was a screen, behind which someone seemed to be stirring. I assumed it was Kenny, the Professor's lovely assistant.

The Professor was sitting at the only dressing table in the room, the lights surrounding the mirror providing most of the illumination. Two of the bulbs were burned out.

"Frank, I haven't seen you since we've got back," the Professor said when he turned to see who had entered. He'd been out of town all summer playing an engagement in the Catskills.

"Sorry, I've been busy. Working on *Death Buys a Condo*. It will be out soon."

"Good for you. What brings you to the Blue Angel? Or have you developed a taste for the art of prestidigitation?"

"Actually, I've come to consult about a case."

"I thought you had given up the P.I. business for a literary career?"

"I have, but I've kind of been dragged into this business against my will."

"I see. Mysterious as always. Just what is it you want to know, Frank?"

"It's kind of confidential."

"I understand," the Professor replied. Shouting towards the screen he asked, "Kenny, could you give us a moment alone?"

"Sure thing, Professor."

A skinny guy in his late twenties appeared from the behind the screen. He was wearing the kind of skimpy costume favored by magician's assistants. When I'd first run into Kenny he'd been a skinny kid stumbling around in fishnet stockings, high heels, and an ill-fitting blonde wig playing the part of the Blue Angel's cigarette girl. Somehow he'd ended up as the Professor's assistant. Considering that he was sawn in half twice a week, I'm not sure that it was an improvement. He still wore fishnet stockings, but his balance seemed to have improved and the Professor had gotten him a much better wig.

I don't think there is anything between the two of them. In the time I've known him, the Professor has never shown any sexual interest one way or the other. Not that I care. Or even inquired. It's none of my business. I think that, remembering his own rough childhood, the Professor has taken a sort of avuncular interest in Kenny and tried to help him out the only way he can.

After Kenny had left, I outlined the details of Black's murder, particularly the part about my appearing in the security video. The Professor looked thoughtful for a moment before responding.

"I take it you're asking my professional opinion as to how it was pulled off?"

"Something like that. I've got to admit that I'm confused as hell about it. Any ideas that you've got would be a big help."

"Okay. Well, stage magic is all about manipulating expectations. One of the oldest dodges in magic is to get two assistants about the same general build and height. You dress them up in identical costumes and have them put on identical wigs, the more attention grabbing, the better. You then put one of the assistants in say a cabinet, swing it around and do the usual mumbo-jumbo, abracadabra and have the other assistant pop out of a trunk on the other side of the stage. The audience is expecting that something is going to happen involving the first assistant, so that's what they think they are seeing. They see the costume, the wig, and they don't bother to look any closer."

"Yeah, I understand that, but in this case there wouldn't have been any expectation that I would just happen to be in the lobby of the apartment building at that time. I'd only been there a couple of times, and the last time was nearly six months ago."

"Don't be so sure, Frank. Think about it for a minute. Who's the top homicide detective in the city? The one who gets all the high profile cases?"

"That would probably be Flannigan," I replied.

"Lt. Flannigan, someone who knows you quite well and who could be expected to recognize you on sight."

"Okay, maybe. But I've seen the security video. The guy in it didn't just look something like me, it was me, or at least close enough to fool a close friend. Hell, it almost would have fooled me."

"We seldom are good judges of our own appearance, Frank. The one person we don't need to recognize is ourselves."

"But it was more than just a passing resemblance," I protested.

"Was it? Let's try to imagine how someone might pull this off. First off, physically there is nothing exceptional about you. You've got an average build; you're just slightly above average in height. There are plenty of men in this city who match those characteristics. Next, you have, shall we say, somewhat unique sartorial tastes, though why your lovely wife puts up with them, I don't know."

"What's wrong with the way I dress?"

Okay, I admit I'm not the world's snappiest dresser. Maybe my suits tend to be a bit rumpled and I usually go around in an old trench coat and a battered fedora. People kind of expect that when you're in the P.I. racket.

"I'm not criticizing you, Frank, just commenting. Remember, we are talking about creating the illusion of you. You take someone of you approximate build, dress them up in the style that is associated with you, and you're halfway there."

"Okay, I see that, but what about my face. There was a clear view of the guy staring right into the camera on the tape."

"That, in itself is suspicious. How many people look up at one of those things? Now, I admit that duplicating your visage presents more of a challenge. You have no real distinguishing feature such as a beard or mustache or prominent scar. Your features, it must be admitted, are remarkably ordinary. But, if we assume the intent was only to fool the security camera—I assume that it was black and white and not color?"

"Yeah."

"So the illusion only had to be sufficient to appear to be you in a black and white image taken from a distance of, let's say six feet or so. It wasn't necessary to maintain the illusion under close scrutiny. You take someone with facial features roughly the same as yours, use some makeup to recreate shadow lines, a eyebrow pencil to alter the brows to match, maybe a little bit of putty to adjust the nose or chin—any good makeup artist could probably handle that without much effort."

I thought over what the Professor had said. His explanation certainly sounded plausible.

"I have to admit, Professor, that what you've said makes me feel better. I was beginning to have my doubts. The video would have been enough to make Flannigan suspect me except for the fact that at the time of the murder I was sitting right next to him watching a basketball game."

"Ah, yes, the unbreakable alibi. That's where the killer made a fatal mistake. He planned for everything except for the fact that at the time of the crime you would be sitting next to the one person the killer was counting on to tie you to the murder."

"Yeah. Just plain dumb luck. I wasn't even planning on going to the game but I happened to get some tickets at the last minute. You've been a big help, Professor. I might want to hook you up with Flannigan so you can explain how it was probably done. That won't be a problem, will it?" These days the Professor is completely legit as far as I know, but I knew his carney past made him uncomfortable around the minions of the law.

"Of course, Frank. Anything to help." He paused for a moment. "Maybe I shouldn't mention it under the circumstances, but there is another possibility."

"I'm not sure I like the sound of that, Professor."

"That's why I hesitate to mention it."

I looked over at the Professor. I could see there was something on his mind.

"Okay, Professor. Go ahead, shoot. What is this possibility that is so dire that you don't want to mention it?"

Again, the Professor looked at me, not the way a normal person would, but as if he could see something others could not. He'd once mentioned something about my aura being unusual. At the time, I thought that it was just part of his spiritualist's patter. Now I wasn't so sure.

"Have you ever heard of *doppelgangers*, Frank?"

"I'm not sure I have. What do you have on your mind?"

"It's a German term. Literally, it means double-goer or double walker, but it refers to a being that is an identical duplicate of someone. It crops up in European folklore and also in literature. Poe wrote a story involving one, 'William Wilson.' Various famous people like John Donne and the poet Shelley are reputed to have seen the doppelgangers of themselves or a loved one. Of course, those may just be stories that became attached to them rather than something that actual occurred."

"So just what does this doppelganger business have to do with me? Or Black's murder, for that matter?"

"In the mythology, doppelgangers are portrayed as something supernatural. They often are associated with death or with bad luck. Sometimes, the doppelganger takes on the role of 'evil twin.' Either possibility seems as though it might be relevant."

"You don't really expect me to believe that I've got an evil twin that is responsible for the murder of Joshua Black, do you?"

"I sincerely hope that is not the case, Frank. That was why I was reluctant to mention it. I concluded, though, that it would be irresponsible on my part not to. We both know that there is something not quite natural about you."

"I don't know what you mean, Professor," I said defensively.

"I think you do. You may not know what it is, but I know you sense it. I can read it in your aura. I told you that the first time we met."

"Excuse me, Professor, but I think you're talking a lot of hooey."

The Professor shrugged. "You're probably right, Frank. Chalk it up to the imaginings of an aging mind if you will. That might be best. But remember, I'm available if you need my help."

That was the problem with the Professor. He was a life-long con-man, trickster, and phony spiritualist, but he was also at heart an honest, caring man who would do anything to help his friends. What he had told me, he had told me because he had thought I needed to know. He might not believe in all the supernatural business, but he didn't *disbelieve* in it either.

I think he recognized the awkwardness of the situation because he quickly changed the subject.

"Are you going to stick around for the show? I've got a couple of new tricks that are worth seeing."

"I'm not sure, Professor. I'll probably have a drink, at least. I should say hi to Jo before I leave, at least."

"Well, then, Frank, till we meet again. And now, if you'll forgive me, I've got to get ready for the show."

Chapter Five

After I left the Professor's dressing room, I was planning to head home, but as walked through the crowd, I heard the emcee announce that Josephine LaTouche would be performing next. It had been a while since I'd seen Jo sing, and after my talk with the Professor I felt that I could use a drink. I headed for an open spot at the bar and ordered a watered down Scotch and soda.

I got my drink just as Jo was taking the stage. Jo has developed a stage presence that is—well, dominating. Of course when you're just under six foot three in high heels and weigh in at nearly two hundred pounds, that's easier to pull off, but Jo managed to do it with a style and grace that seemed natural. That night Jo was wearing a sleek-fitting floor-length red evening gown, black opera gloves and a blonde wig that curled around her shoulders.

As she strolled over to the microphone stand in the center of the stage, a spot light from the back of the room followed her path. Unlike some of the talent at the Blue Angel, Jo doesn't affect a mincing gait or an exaggerated sashay; she just walks slowly and deliberately.

It was obvious that most of the crowd knew what was coming because they quieted down in anticipation.

With a caressing touch on the microphone Jo greeted the crowd, "Thank you all for coming to see me tonight," echoing the line by Mae West. Jo doesn't use a falsetto in her act; instead her voice is a husky tenor with a texture like a fine whiskey, smooth and rough all at the same time.

Jo nodded to the band, a trio of piano, drums and bass with a guy that doubles on sax and clarinet as needed. I can't remember the name of the song, I'm not sure I had ever heard it before, but it was all about love and longing, the kind of material that Jo does best. When she was done, she stood for a moment, her head bowed before the mike waiting for the applause. The Blue Angel isn't that big of a place, and the crowd was a little sparse that night, but, you wouldn't have known that from the response they gave Jo.

A couple of show tunes and standards followed, not as good maybe as the first tune, but good enough to please the crowd. She followed that with "Crazy," the Willie Nelson song that Patsy Cline had made famous. That had some of the audience standing on their feet.

When the house quieted down again, she launched into a medley of thirties torch songs, doing a verse or two of each song and then letting the band vamp into the next tune. There was a polish to her act that none of the other performers at the Blue Angel are close to matching, which is why she's become the headliner.

During the week, Jo usually limits her sets to forty-five minutes or so to save her voice, or so she claims, but there is one song that she always includes as a finale. I think the audience would revolt and tear up the joint if she didn't.

"Lili Marlene" has become Jo's signature tune. Unless you've seen her sing it, it's hard to understand why. It's a simple tune from a bygone era. The arrangement is spare, with only the piano for backing. At the Blue Angel, they lower the lights so that there is only the spot on Jo. There is a pause, and then she sings the first phrase without the piano, a hard trick for any performer to pull off. The first verse is sung in English to draw in the audience, then Jo switches to German. The language of the final refrain depends on Jo's mood and that of the crowd.

The final note died, the spot went out, there was a moment of silence and then the clapping began. The lights came back on, Jo blew kisses at the audience, then at the band, and then back at the audience.

There were some shouts for an encore, but Jo never sings one. She knows when to leave the audience on a high. Instead she made her bow and then the stage lights went out.

Next thing I knew, Jo was standing next to me.

"Frank, it's been awhile. Care to buy a girl a drink?"

I caught the bartender's attention. He nodded in understanding.

"You were great as usual, Jo," I said.

"You're too kind, Frank. Are you slumming or did you come special to see me?"

"Actually, I had some business to discuss with the Professor."

"You disappoint me, Frank. To lead a girl on and then dash her hopes like that—" When Jo is in persona, she has a habit of flirting shamelessly, particularly when she knows her target is straight. We knew each other well enough, that it had become part of the ritual.

Up close, some of the illusion that Jo creates vanishes. If you look closely, you can see the hint of a five o'clock shadow that the makeup doesn't cover up, and a dozen other details that aren't apparent when Jo is on stage.

The bartender brought Jo's drink, a flute of champagne, maybe not the best champagne, but at least it promoted the image.

"What did you want with the Professor, Frank? The old man is a dear, but—"

"I wanted to ask him how a trick could be pulled off. For a case I'm working on."

"I thought you'd gotten out of the detective racket, Frank. What will Janet say?" Somehow, against type, Janet and Jo have become friends. Jo even sang at our wedding.

"It was her suggestion that I talk to the Professor."

"Well, Janet is one smart dame. She must have had her reasons. Thanks for the drink, Frank, but I've got to mingle with my adoring fans. Next time, bring Janet."

"I'll do that."

Jo set her drink on the bar and wandered off. She makes a point of making personal contact with the audience, particularly the regulars, which I guess is part of her appeal.

The Professor's act was next, so I decided to hang around for a bit. The crowd started to thin out, though a few new customers trickled in. For the most part, they looked like the kind that would actually visit the Blue Angel for the magic show. Not that many places have live stage magic these days.

The Professor came on and started his act. He's an old school magician, no rock music or flashing lights, just a guy in a tuxedo and top hat. For starters, he pulled a rabbit out of that hat. There was a moment of embarrassed silence which the Professor broke by saying, "Now that we've got that out of the way, let's get down to some real magic." That got a laugh and seemed to warm up the audience.

He came down onto the floor and did some close up stuff, cards, balls, all the old tricks. The Blue Moon is small enough that people could see what was going on no matter where they sat. The Professor has been doing what he does a long time and he's gotten pretty good at it. None of it was particularly new, but no one seemed to know how he was doing it, either. There was one table with three young guys who were following his every move intently. I figured them for magicians in training.

After about ten minutes of the small stuff, he got back on the stage. Kenny came out pushing a small table. I had to admit that from a distance he made a pretty good "lovely assistant." His costume seemed to fit better and he no longer was unsteady as he walked across the stage in his high heels. There were some flashier tricks, puffs of smoke and flashes of light, disappearing boxes and reappearing pigeons.

Finally, it came time for the final trick, the one where Kenny get's sawn in two. I'd seen it up close once, and even then, I couldn't figure out how it was done. Kenny's gotten to be a better actor, too. He had just the right expression of uncertainty as he climbed into the cabinet. Or at least I think he was acting. The Professor ran through the usual shtick of tickling the feet to show the audience that it really was just one person in the box and then asked two of the apprentice magicians to come up on stage to assist.

There was a great big two-handed lumberjack saw. I knew from experience that it was real. He had the two guys from the audience saw through the box. Kenny looked like he had fainted. I thought one of the amateur magicians was going to as well when the Professor separated the two halves of the box.

That's the point in the act when the Professors starts to walk off stage and when the emcee comes rushing on the Professor says that he promised to saw a woman in half but he'd never said anything about putting her back together. I knew how the act would end, so I got up and left.

As I drove home, I got to thinking about the line between illusion and reality. After all, which really had more impact on the world, Jo's stage performance, or her "real" life? It was a question with a lot of implications, some of which I didn't really want to delve into.

I was glad to get home with Janet.

CHAPTER SIX

I've kept the old office from my days as a P.I. Having an office gives me someplace to go during the day and makes it feel like I'm still working, a feeling that is sometimes hard to get writing. I find that it's more conducive to my writing than the apartment which is too comfortable and has way too many distractions, not the least of which is Janet. The décor of the apartment, which is modern and stylish doesn't seem to fit in with the hard-boiled noir vibe, either.

The office is on the third floor of an old commercial building, the kind of place where the elevator doesn't work half of the time, the hallways are lit by dim milk white globes hanging from the ceiling and the wood of the wainscoting has turned dark from age and grime. The door to the office has frosted glass with my name painted on it in thick, black letters. The words "Private Detective" have been scratched off and replaced by "Writer" in lettering that doesn't quite match. I thought that that was a nice touch. Most of the furniture inside dates from the thirties, matching the vintage of the building and somehow just feels right. It's a great place to write about murder.

Even though it now says "Writer" on the door, people still wander in occasionally thinking I'm still in the P.I. racket. Mostly I try to discourage them gently and point them in some other direction, unless they happen to be an old acquaintance or have an interesting story to tell, or I'm just plain bored with staring at a blank sheet of paper sitting in the battered typewriter on my desk. Sometimes I can help them; sometimes I just give them a sympathetic ear to fill. All in all, it's not such a bad life.

I was sitting in the office debating about whether to jot down some ideas for future books or make another foray into Handler's effects when Flannigan knocked on the glass of the door. He didn't bother to wait for an invitation, but just walked in. I suppose I should lock the door, but somehow I never seem to get around to it.

"Have a seat," I said by way of a greeting.

Flannigan pulled up one of the chairs and parked himself facing the desk. As he did so, he eyed the half empty bottle of rye sitting next to the typewriter, raising an eyebrow as if to ask "a little early in the day, isn't it?" The truth is, the bottle has become a bit of set dressing, something to maintain the mood. If I really feel the need for a drink, there's a nice quiet tavern down on the corner. Sometimes, when I'm immersed in my writing, I'll pour a couple of fingers into one of the glasses I keep in the top right hand drawer, but then I usually ignore it as I pound on the typewriter keys. More often than not, I end up pouring it back into the bottle. After all, it would be a shame to waste good whiskey, or cheap rye, for that matter. Mostly, it's a matter of maintaining a certain image, even if I'm the only one watching.

"What can I do for you, Flannigan? I'm kind of busy."

"I can see that," he said, his voice dripping with sarcasm. "It's about the Black case. I was wondering if you've been able to make any sense of it. I sure haven't."

"Well, seeing as you've asked, I went to see the Professor last night—"

"Longwell? That old charlatan? What's he got to do with it?"

"Nothing, really. It's just that if that business of the guy in the security footage was some kind of a trick, I thought he might have some idea as to how it was pulled off."

"I see. And did he?"

"As a matter of fact, he did." I went on to relate what the Professor had told me about dressing up someone my size in a coat and hat like the ones I wore. I didn't think it necessary to go into the bit about the *doppelganger* which sounded even crazier in the light of day than it had the previous night.

Flannigan thought about it for a bit then asked, "You really think that's what happened?"

"It certainly seems plausible. After all, we both know that it wasn't me, no matter what it may have looked like. So what other explanation could there be other than it was someone impersonating me? After all, I'm pretty sure I don't have a twin brother."

"What about a cousin?" Flannigan asked in his best police detective voice.

"Not that I know of, though I have to admit my knowledge of my family tree is a bit sketchy." I didn't mention the fact that I don't even really remember my parents clearly, other than that I'm pretty sure I had some.

"So you think some guy dressed up like you with a bit of grease paint or whatever could fool the both of us?"

"It's the only logical explanation. Remember, neither one of us saw the murderer in the flesh. We only saw a black and white recording."

"I'm still not convinced," Flannigan responded.

"Do you have a better explanation? If you do, I'd like to hear it."

It was pretty clear that Flannigan didn't have any better ideas, though it was also plain that he wasn't completely satisfied with mine. He sat for a moment staring out the grimy office window at the fog outside.

"You know, Frank, that if what you are suggesting is true, it raises another question."

"What's that, Flannigan?"

"Why would someone go to all the trouble of impersonating you just to kill Black? After all, all he would really have to do is disguise himself so as not to look like himself. There's no reason for him to bring you into the business at all. Is there?"

"What are you implying?"

"The only reason to impersonate you would be to implicate you in Black's murder. Who have you pissed off, Frank?"

"Lately? Probably lots of people over the years. Not that I can bring any to mind, at least that would have it in for me enough to kill Black and frame me for it. Maybe the killer just wanted to divert your attention so that you'd waste your time checking into my alibis or whatever."

"If that was his intention, he could have disguised himself as anything. He could have put on a fake eye-patch and perched a parrot on his shoulder and we'd have wasted days looking for a pirate in a trench coat. No, Frank. The fact that it was you the killer impersonated means that he had a reason for doing so. All we have to do is figure out why."

"Sure. Of course, you're forgetting something."

"What's that?"

"If this killer had it in for me, why did he bother to murder Josh Black? Why didn't he just bump me off direct, instead?"

"Okay. Good question. Why would anyone want to knock off Black? I didn't know the guy, but I've read some of his books. I thought they were pretty good. You'd met him before. What kind of guy was he?"

"Pretty nice, from what I knew of him. When he found out that I was trying to become a writer he was encouraging and helped me out with some tips. The people that I've talked to that knew him all seemed to feel the same way, that he was a pretty straight shooter. Not the kind of guy that made enemies. Not much of a motive, is it Flannigan?"

"No, I guess it isn't. So what do the two of you have in common?"

"Not much, except for the fact that we both wrote detective novels. Rather, I've written two and he'd written a couple of dozen. And my second one hasn't even come out yet. Besides, what kind of person would go around bumping off mystery writers?"

"I don't know," Flannigan said with a shrug. "Maybe another mystery writer?"

"Seems pretty farfetched as a motive, if you ask me."

"Okay. Let's look at it from another angle. You were tied up in the Handler case. Another mystery writer, I'll point out. Did Black know Handler?"

"I know that they'd met professionally. Awards dinners, things like that. I don't think they were close friends, but as far as I know they got along alright. I can ask Janet. She'd know more about that sort of thing. Remember, I never met Handler when he was alive."

"Okay, is there anyone Black might have written about that got him on their wrong side, someone that you might have crossed paths with in the past?"

"Black never wrote any true crime stuff that I know of. And given the libel laws, I would have thought that Black would have been pretty careful not to make any of his characters appear to be too identifiable with real people. That really wasn't his style, anyway. At least, I've never heard about anyone that had a beef with Black on that account."

"Which brings us back to you, Frank. Maybe you were the target all along, and Black was murdered just to create a high profile case to tie you into. Who would want to do you harm?"

"Honestly, Flannigan, I can't think of anyone. It's not like I'm rich or anything. I'm pretty much of a nobody. Up until the Handler case, I was a two-bit P.I. with a cheap office. Now, I'm a two-bit writer with a cheap office. Hell, the only thing worth anything in my life is Janet."

"So, anyone who might want to get you out of the way so they could make a move on her?"

"Not that I know of. Before me, she was with Handler, and she's not the kind of woman who would have had something going on the side. She just isn't made that way." The last I said a little heatedly.

"Forget I mentioned it, Frank."

Flannigan stared up at the ceiling for a moment, tilting his head to the point where I thought his hat might fall off.

"Okay, Frank. How about this. Maybe the killer didn't have a beef with Black and you specifically. Maybe he's just got a problem with mystery writers in general, and he's trying to knock them off two by two."

"That's crazy, Flannigan. That's the kind of plot line you'd only find in a mystery novel, and probably not a very good one at that."

"Yeah, you're probably right. This case has got me going nowhere fast. I'd better be moving along. If you think of anything, you'll let me know, right?"

"You'll be the first to hear about it, Flannigan."

With that, the lieutenant got up and walked out of the office.

Chapter Seven

A few days after Flannigan dropped by, Sally Johnson was found dead in her apartment. Sally had been an old time newspaper woman who could have come straight out of "The Front Page." She had been a great old dame who looked like your grandmother, that is if your grandma chain-smoked, drank her bourbon straight, and had a poker face that would have been the envy of any professional card shark.

Sally had started working for the *Tribune-Gazette* back in the 1930's when it was still just the *Tribune,* and the newspaper game was a man's world. Even back then she hadn't been satisfied with covering flower shows, the social set, and other feminine things, and when most of the male reporters went away to the war, either as correspondents or to fight, she'd become the papers lead crime reporter. After the war ended, she had refused to be shunted aside, working the crime beat until she retired. Along the way she'd written a baker's dozen of police procedurals admired mostly for their graphic descriptions of crime scenes and corpses, a realism that came from experience, and for their less than flattering depictions of the inner workings of a big city police force. She'd never had the commercial success of a writer like Josh Black, but her novels had earned the respect of the critics and other writers alike.

I was sitting at home watching TV with Janet when Flannigan called. All that he said over the phone was that I'd "better get over here," and gave me an address.

I put on my hat and coat and drove over. It was a couple of days after Christmas, decorations were still hanging from the lamp posts, snowflakes, candles, and wreathes, bobbing in the wind. It had snowed the night before, a couple of inches, but not enough to make the streets slick.

The address had sounded vaguely familiar when Flannigan had given it to me over the phone, but I didn't place it until I pulled up in front. It was an older but still respectable four story apartment building, the kind of place where the residents were either spinsters or widows who'd come there to die. I'd been there once before, to a poker game in Sally Johnson's apartment. I had a premonition, and it wasn't a good one.

The uniform watching the door gave me directions that confirmed my suspicions. I rode the elevator up in silence and got off it into the usual crime scene pandemonium of fingerprint technicians, detectives, and a couple of guys from the M.E. waiting patiently with a gurney to take the body away. Down the hall there was a little old lady who kept peeking out the door of her apartment and a uniformed policeman who patiently kept asking her to please go back inside. When the old lady saw me, she ducked back into her doorway, but not before whispering something in the cop's ear. The cop looked in my direction and gave me the fish eye.

I was expected, and no one tried to stop me when I entered the apartment.

The apartment was by no means as swank as Black's, just a small living room and a smaller dining area with a tiny galley kitchen off to the side. A short hallway towards the back had a bedroom and bathroom opening onto it.

The walls of the living room were covered with photos. They weren't the usual old lady kitsch of nieces and nephews and dead relatives, these were mostly pictures of men in the dapper suits of the 40's and 50's being arrested and crime scene photos that Sally had taken during her working years. One picture of Sally showed her standing between two FBI agents holding a Thompson submachine gun almost as big as she was. The only sign of domesticity was a tiny Christmas tree perched on a table in the corner, its single strand of lights winking festively.

Flannigan was standing in the kitchen looking down at the corpse. Sally was lying on the floor, a knife stuck in her back. The pool of blood on the vinyl flooring was surprisingly small, but then she'd been a small woman, maybe five feet two, thin and frail, looking every one of her seventy some years. The years of chain-smoking, bourbon whiskey, and late hours had taken their toll, and she hadn't been in good health the last few years. Not that that had stopped her. Her last book had come out the year before. It had been a doozey, too.

There was a bottle of Southern Comfort sitting on the counter along with two glasses, a bottle of bitters, and an ice cube tray half full of water. When she hadn't been drinking her whiskey straight, Sally had been fond of Old Fashioneds. I noticed that there was an empty slot in the knife block next to the stove that looked like it might have been the home of the knife in Sally's back.

"What happened?" I asked when Flannigan glanced up and saw me.

"Not sure yet. Her neighbor down the hall got worried when she hadn't seen the victim for a day, knocked on the door and noticed that it wasn't latched. She opened it up to check on her friend. That's when she discovered the body. It must have been quite a shock. We're lucky we don't have two corpses on our hands."

He related all this in that matter of fact manner policemen have, but I could sense the tension behind the measured cadence of his voice.

I responded with, "I knew her, Flannigan. She was a swell old lady."

"I figured as much. I knew her, too, at least by sight from when she was still with the *Tribune*." As an afterthought he added, "She wrote mysteries, too, didn't she?"

"Police procedurals," I corrected, "but yeah, she was a writer. A good one, too."

"Is that how you knew her?"

"Yeah, someone introduced me. I think it might have been Josh Black. I played poker with her a couple of times, once here."

"Who else was in the game?" Flannigan asked, his pencil and notebook in his hands.

"Black, another writer whose name I can't remember at the moment and a couple of old reporter types. I can probably come up with their names if I think about it for awhile."

"You do that, Frank," Flannigan said, his voice suddenly hard and professional.

"What's the deal, Flannigan? Was there more security video of me?"

"No. This building doesn't rate a camera. But one of the tenants mentioned seeing someone in a trench coat and fedora about the time the M.E. figures the murder happened. She only saw him from the back as he was getting on the elevator, so she won't be able to give us an I.D."

"What time was that?" I had an idea of where Flannigan was going with this.

"Last night. About eight."

"I've got an alibi, Flannigan. Janet dragged me to one of her charity things. There were probably hundreds of people there that saw me. We sat next to a couple that she knows. The wife works in the D.A.'s office."

"It figures," Flannigan responded, suddenly sounding tired. "Sorry about the attitude, Frank. Just doing my business."

"Don't worry. I understand. I didn't know Sally that well, but I know she didn't deserve to die like this."

"No one does."

"For what it's worth, I noticed a couple of things that might be of help."

"What's that?" Flannigan responded, suddenly attentive.

"The first thing is that it looks like Sally was making drinks when she was killed. Two of them. There were two glasses on the counter. You don't usually make drinks for someone who breaks in."

"So she knew whoever it was?"

"That's what I'm thinking. It fits in with Black's killing which happened in his office. He didn't normally invite strangers into there. Or turn his back on them. I'd say that he knew his killer as well. And in neither case was there any sign of a struggle."

"That's a good lead, Frank. Something that we can follow up on. There can't be that many people that they both knew."

"Probably more than you might think, Flannigan. Sally and Black were pretty public figures each in their own way. There are probably hundreds of people that they were both acquainted with."

"Still, it's something. You said you noticed a couple of things. What was the other?"

"The choice of murder weapons. In both instances, the weapon was something picked up from the victim's apartment. Almost as if the murders were spontaneous. In Black's case it was the award statue that was sitting on a shelf in his office. In Sally's case, it was a kitchen knife from the block sitting next to the stove. Like the killer just chose whatever was handy. That's pretty unusual. If you go to someone's place planning to kill them, most times you'll bring your own weapon with you, something like a pistol or a switchblade, rather than counting on being able to find something at the opportune moment. At least, that's the way I'd write it in a mystery."

"I see you're point, Frank. It does seem to be a pretty odd M.O."

"The whole thing is screwy. If someone is planning these murders, they're not doing a very good job of it."

"Then you think that both of these murders are connected?"

"It doesn't make sense any other way. I can see someone flying off the handle, maybe at something said, one time. But for it to happen twice? That seems a bit much to be just a coincidence."

Flannigan mulled that over for a moment.

"So what gives, Frank? Why would someone knock off an old woman like this? Or Black, for that matter. Do you really think it has something to do with their being writers?"

"I wish I knew, Flannigan. I wish I knew."

Chapter Eight

What we had both left unsaid was the question, "Who's next?" Fortunately, at least if the targets of the mystery assassin were authors of detective fiction, there weren't that many in town. I only knew of a couple of others, three if I included myself. As I rode the elevator down on the way out it occurred to me that I was both a prime suspect and on the short list of potential victims.

I was still thinking about the question as I sat in my office the next day. I should have been trying to write something, but I just wasn't in the mood. The murders of two people that I had known and liked seemed more important. When it came right down to it, so did my avoiding being added to the list.

I did what the detectives in British mysteries always seem to do in that sort of situation, I made a list. I've always thought lists were a gimmick authors used to pad out books, but I didn't have any better ideas going for me. It wasn't going to be very long, at least if I confined it to the local detective writers that I knew. This town isn't really a hotbed of authors, not like New York or L.A. This is what I came up with:

Ezekial Handler – previously deceased. His death probably had no bearing on the current case.

Josh Black – deceased, writer of crime novels, 1st victim

Sally Johnson – deceased, former newspaper woman and writer of police procedurals, 2nd victim

Max Tulley – still alive. Novels feature a hard-boiled private investigator. Tulley was sort of a mid-western Ross MacDonald.

Harold Gaskell – still alive, I as far as I knew. In his eighties. Wrote a few detective novels in the 40's, but he hadn't written anything in decades.

Karen Frickle – still alive. Wrote "cozy mysteries" under the pen-name Millicent de Bracey.

Frank Slade – still alive. Former P.I. First book, *Murder After Midnight*. Second book *Death Buys a Condo* about to be released.

As far as I was aware, those were all of the professional writers of detective fiction in town. At least it was all the ones that I had met. There were a couple of other writers and writer wannabes that hung around the fringes, but none of them had been published, at least in the detective genre.

Gaskell seemed a long shot. He'd been out of the business for a long time and as far as I knew didn't really have any connections with either of the victims.

Max I knew fairly well. He'd been one of the players at the poker game at Sally Johnson's apartment. He'd been close friends with Josh Black as well. He'd been the one who had delivered the eulogy at Josh Black's wake the night Sally had been murdered.

I had been introduced to Karen Frickle once at some charity event Janet had dragged me to on the basis of us both being writers. When she discovered that I was a former P.I. and wrote in the hard-boiled vein, she'd suddenly seen an old friend that she just had to talk to. It was probably just as well; as writers, we had nothing in common. Her cozy mysteries took place in quaint cottages in the English countryside. Her characters drank tea, not whiskey. Murder, in her world, usually took the form of poison, or electrocution and never, ever involved shootings, stabbings, or bludgeoning. As far as I knew, there were no connections between Frickle and Sally or Black. They had run in different circles.

As long as I was making up lists, I thought I might as well make one of the poker players at Sally's apartment. The two murder victims had both been there, which made as much sense as someone going around knocking off detective writers. In addition to Sally and Josh, there had been myself, Max Tulley and two old-time newspaper men that Sally knew; Fred Sandage and Bob Cleveland.

Somehow, I couldn't see either Sandage or Cleveland as killers. Fred was a heavyset guy whose nickname was "Sandwich." He smiled a lot and was always telling jokes, some of which were even clean. He mostly covered politics and city hall. Bob Cleveland had grown up in the inner city and had been a star basketball player in high school. He'd been good enough to get a scholarship, but too short to make the jump to the pros. Instead, he'd gotten a degree in journalism and ended up as the sports reporter for the *Tribune-Gazette*. From his stuff that I had read in the paper, he was pretty good at that. He had talked a lot at the poker game about writing a sports novel, but I don't think he'd ever done anything about it. The others at the poker game who knew him better had made it seem like he was always doing that. Sandage and Cleveland were both in their mid-fifties and had known Sally for decades.

Of the four surviving poker players, on the surface, Max made the most likely killer, but only because of his past. He didn't look much like the private eyes he wrote about. He was maybe five-foot seven and weighed a hundred and forty. He didn't talk about it much, but he'd served in Vietnam and earned a Purple Heart and a Bronze Star. If you looked into his eyes at the wrong moment, it wouldn't be too hard to imagine him shoving a knife into someone. The problem with that theory was that Max would never have committed murders as sloppy as Sally's and Black's. He'd have planned it out ahead of time and come fully prepared. I'd read a couple of his books and they were strong on detail. Besides, he didn't have any motive that I could think of.

And that's what it came down to, motive. If the two murders were linked, who had a motive and what was it? All of the people on my lists really seemed to have liked and respected each other. As far as I knew, none of them had any sort of business dealings with the others outside of the poker games and those had been played for nickels and dimes. And as for sex? It was conceivable that Sally might have been a heart throb in her younger days, but those days had ended with the Roosevelt administration. I could probably rule out enmity, greed, and sex as motives. What did that leave?

It was possible that Karen Frickle might have wanted to get rid of Josh and Sally because their mysteries were anything but cozy, but if that was the case, she probably would have sent them arsenic laced tea cakes or something.

It was pretty clear that all this wild speculation was getting me nowhere fast. Was there anything more I could do?

It occurred to me that at least I could warn Max to be on his guard. I reached for the phone and gave him a call.

"Max Tulley," he answered after a couple of rings.

"Hi, Max. Frank Slade."

"Oh. Hi Frank. Sorry about the other night, but I had made previous plans."

"The other night?" I asked in confusion. "What about it?"

"You called and said you wanted to come over and talk about your next novel. Don't you remember?"

"No. Not really. Are you sure it was me?"

"It sounded like you. Whoever it was said their name was Frank. I guess that I just assumed it was you. You're the only Frank I know."

"Sorry, but it wasn't me."

"Well, I guess it isn't important then. What did you want?"

"Something has come up. In relationship to Sally's and Josh Black's murders. I've kind of been working with Flannigan on the case."

"Are the police getting anywhere with it? They were both good friends of mine, and I hope they get whoever is responsible."

"Not so far. But there's kind of a wild theory going around."

"What's that?"

"That Josh and Sally were targeted because they were mystery writers. If they're right that means—"

"That means I might be next," Max interrupted.

"Yeah. Yeah, after Josh and Sally, you're probably the best known detective writer in the city."

"Thanks, I guess. Sort of a crazy idea, though, isn't it? I mean, who would go around bumping off a bunch of writers?"

"Yeah. Like I say, it's just one of those wild ideas that come up when nothing else makes sense. But, all the same, I thought I should warn you to be on your guard."

"Yeah. Thanks for calling," he responded. Then after a moment he added, "You're serious about this, aren't you, Frank."

"Yeah. Kind of. The police haven't released details yet, but in both cases it looks as if the victims knew the killer. They were both killed when their backs were turned. Sally was stabbed with one of her own kitchen knives while she was making drinks for the killer and herself."

"Sheesh. You're kidding, aren't you, Frank?"

"No. Afraid not. Black was killed when someone picked up one of his awards and bashed the back of his skull in."

"Thanks for the info, Frank. What about you? Are you on the list, too?"

"I'm not sure. I'm not even sure there is a list. But I just thought I should let you know—in case. So be careful."

"I'll do that."

"And Max—"

"Yes?"

"If I should come over—make sure it's me before you let me in."

"What's that supposed to mean, Frank?"

"Probably nothing. It's just this idea that Flannigan has, that the killer might be impersonating me."

"You're kidding? That's like an idea out of a bad detective story. Like something what's-his-name, Frenzel would come up with."

Jerry Frenzel was this wannabe mystery writer that hung around. He didn't have any talent, but he was always trying to foist off manuscripts on other writers to look at. He'd even shoved one at me once after he'd found out I'd written *Murder After Midnight*. I'd made the mistake of reading a few pages. It had been terrible.

"Just be careful, Max. Okay?"

"Sure thing, Frank. Thanks for calling." Then he hung up.

I thought about calling Karen Frickle, but decided against it. In the first place, she'd think I was crazy, and second—well I've never been that fond of cozy mysteries.

I did decide to call Flannigan. I'd promised him the names of the other players at the poker game. I read him the list over the phone along with thumbnail descriptions of each of them. I even included Frickle's name to make up for not calling her.

"Thanks, Frank. Though, from what you say, none of these people look like suspects."

"Probably not."

"I've got one good bit of news, though. At least for you."

"What's that?"

"The check of the fingerprints on the statue at Black's came back. They weren't yours." I knew my fingerprints were on file, because they'd been taken when I applied for my P.I. license. I'd also known that Flannigan would have them checked as a matter of course.

"That's a relief. Not that I don't have an alibi with a credible witness."

"Funny thing, though. When he was checking them against yours, he noticed something."

"What's that?"

"The M.E. figured out that whoever struck the blow that killed Black was left handed. You're right handed, right? Well, the prints on the statue confirm that the killer was a lefty. The statue was held in the left hand."

"Yeah. That makes sense."

"It's just that—well, the prints on the statue, from a left hand, look a lot like the prints on your right hand—but only if they'd been reversed. Like in a mirror. The fingerprint guy said he'd never seen anything like it before."

"But there's no way they could have been mine?"

"No. He was pretty clear on that. It's just one of those odd coincidences, I guess. A one in a billion thing."

"Anything else?"

"No. Not at the moment. I'll keep in touch."

After he hung up I kept thinking about what Flannigan had told me about the fingerprints. For some reason, what he had said should have meant something to me, but I couldn't figure out what.

Chapter Nine

I was late for dinner, which when you have a wife that looks and cooks like Janet is inexcusable. What made it worse was the fact that Janet didn't pout or complain. She had already had a glass from the bottle of wine that was on the table, but that was certainly understandable. She fussed around in the kitchen a bit and served the meal without comment.

To say that I was distracted during dinner would be an understatement. Thinking back, I can't even remember what it was that we ate, which also in inexcusable. I know that I didn't make much conversation.

Janet waited until the end of the meal before asking, "What's wrong, Frank?"

"What makes you think that something's wrong?" I replied distractedly.

"Well, for one thing, you hardly said a word during dinner. For another, you just picked at your food. That's not like you, Frank."

She wasn't nagging. Janet doesn't nag. Not usually, at least. And she wasn't in this case. As I said earlier, she's the perfect woman. I could tell that she was concerned, and I was being a heel for taking it out on her.

"It's these murders, Josh Black and Sally Johnson. I knew them both. Hell, I liked them both."

"I understand that, Frank. I liked both of them, too. Especially, Sally. She was a great old lady." I sometimes forget that Janet had been part of the mystery writer's scene a lot longer than I have because of her relationship to Handler. Janet continued, "But it's a police matter, Frank. It's not your business. You're not even a private detective anymore, Frank. Shouldn't you let Lt. Flannigan take care of it?"

"Flannigan's at as much of a loss as I am. Nothing makes sense about the murders. There's no obvious motive. Nothing really ties the two victims together except for the fact that they both wrote detective novels. That, and the fact that the killer seems to bear an uncanny resemblance to yours truly."

"There's something more, though, isn't there? Something you're not telling me."

That's what it came down to. With a woman like Janet you've got to tell the truth, because if you don't you risk screwing it up so bad that you can't put things back together again. The problem was, there *were* some things that I'd never told Janet. Like the last letter that I'd gotten from Handler, the one where he claimed that we were all, Janet, Flannigan, Jo, myself, even Armand O'Hara, the guy who ran the newsstand, we were all just constructs, the products of some magic hoodoo that Handler had done to avenge his murder. It didn't matter if it was true or not, and when you said it out loud I had to admit that it seemed pretty improbable. But how could I tell Janet something like that? That she might just be a fantasy that Handler had cooked up with his typewriter and a little mojo. I couldn't risk what it might do to her. Not having seen what it did to me. After I'd gotten the letter, I'd half way believed it. Handler had been a pretty convincing writer when he wanted to. But it had come damned close to destroying me. How could I risk inflicting that same fate on Janet? It would be better to lose her.

So, I did what any red-blooded man would do, I lied—or at least tried to deflect the discussion.

"You're right. There is something, something more. I talked to Max Tully today."

Janet didn't say anything. She just raised an eyebrow.

"I had wanted to warn him—"

"Warn him? Against what?" Janet asked sharply.

"Flannigan's got this theory. It's pretty far out there, but so far it's the only thing that makes sense. That maybe Josh Black and Sally had been targeted because they were mystery writers. If it was true, Max might be the next likely target. I just wanted to let him know so that he'd be on his guard."

"I understand that, Frank. But if someone is targeting mystery writers, doesn't that make you a target as well?" You have to remember that this was coming from someone who had plugged a guy between the eyes with a slug from a .45 automatic to save my miserable hide.

"I don't think that I'm in the same kind of danger, Janet. It's not like I'm famous like Josh and Sally were—or Max. I'm just a novice waiting for his second book to come out." I didn't add that the killer wouldn't be able to fool me the way he had with Josh and Sally. If he *was* impersonating me, I was pretty sure that I'd know he wasn't me. At least I hoped so.

"Still, Frank—just be careful, alright?"

"Don't worry about me. I know how to take care of myself."

"Sure you do, Frank. That's why I had to come rescue you the last time you got yourself into a mess."

I've said that Janet the perfect woman. That doesn't mean that she can't be sarcastic when she feels like it.

"Point taken. I'll be careful."

"There's something more, though, isn't there?"

This was where it was going to get dicey.

"You know how I told you that the surveillance camera at Black's apartment building caught someone who looked a lot like me?"

"Yes. Didn't you say the Professor had an explanation for that?"

"Yeah, but that's not the point. At Sally's place, one of her neighbors caught a glimpse of the back of a man who may have been the killer. He was wearing a trench coat and a hat a lot like the one that I wear. It looks like the killer may be trying to impersonate me."

"But the police know that it wasn't you? Right?"

"Sure. That's not a problem. After all, I've got Flannigan as an alibi for Josh's death, and the fingerprints they picked up are definitely not mine. But what I'm leading up to is that this guy may be using his ability to impersonate me to get close to his victims. That was one of the things that I wanted to warn Max about."

"You don't mean to say this man looks enough like you to fool your friends, are you?"

"He looks enough like me that Josh let him into his office. Enough like me that Sally turned her back on him to make him a drink. Maybe he wouldn't fool anyone for long who really knew me, but it looks like he might be able to pass for me long enough to get someone to turn their back on him. And that's all it would take."

"That's awful, Frank."

"Yeah, I know. The thing is, when I called Max, he apologized about not being available the other night when I called saying that I wanted to come over and talk to him."

"When was this?" Janet asked in surprise.

"The other night. But the point is, I didn't make that call."

"Then you think it was the killer?"

"I think it's a possibility. I think there's a good chance that if Max hadn't had a prior engagement, this city would be short one more writer of detective fiction, and they're getting to be in short supply as it is. Do you understand now why I was distracted at dinner?"

"Of course, Frank. You've got a lot on your mind."

"Good. But Janet—"

"Yes?"

"I want you to be careful. Do you understand? I want you to be sure that it's me the next time you see me."

"Sure, honey," Janet replied in a tone that sounded like she was humoring me.

"I'm not joking about this, Janet," I said sharply.

"Don't you think I'd know if it were you, Frank?"

"Would you? Even if he just fooled you for a few seconds, it might be enough for him to do something."

Janet could tell that I was serious about it. "You really think I'm in danger?"

"I don't know, Janet. I haven't figured out yet what's motivating this guy. Just don't turn your back on me next time we meet, not until you're sure that it really is me."

"I understand, Frank. And remember, I can take care of myself, too."

That's one of things that I love about Janet. Once she grasped the situation there was no backtalk, no arguing, she just accepted the situation.

After that, I helped Janet clean up in the kitchen. She usually tells me not to bother, so I don't, but that night I didn't want to leave her alone, even just in the other room. She didn't seem to mind.

After she went to bed, I sat up with a glass of Scotch, thinking to myself what a great thing I had going, and what a shame it would be to screw it up. The perfect wife, the perfect life, I had it made. It really didn't matter what Handler had said in his last letter. For all I knew, they had been the ramblings of a man going off his rocker, either that, or Handler facing his impending doom, had descended into some kind of fantasy world. So maybe he had been able to predict how things had turned out. Maybe he had predicted them because he had been nudging them along all the time, setting in motion a train of events just as if they were a plot in one of his books. It didn't matter whether magic or sorcery had been involved. What mattered was the here and now. That was the reality of things for me. To believe anything else would be madness.

I finished my drink and went to bed where I knew what awaited me.

Chapter Ten

They held a wake for Sally Johnson's the next evening. She hadn't had any family to speak of, but the arrangements had been made by some of her old newspaper colleagues. Despite the lack of family, a big turnout had been expected and they'd booked the funeral parlors biggest room. Even with that, the crowd ended up spilling out into the corridor. I'm not sure how many of those in attendance were real friends, but Sally had been a fixture in town for so long that anyone associated with crime or the newspaper business had showed up as a mark of respect.

As Sally would have wished, it was anything but a somber event. Bob Cleveland was sitting at an upright piano while Fred Sandage and a couple of ex-reporters tried to work their way through "Danny Boy. Sally hadn't been Irish, and Cleveland certainly wasn't, but I guess all newspapermen are at least honorary Irish. I think it has something to do with the whiskey.

I recognized the city editor of the *Tribune-Gazette*. He was holding a scotch and soda in one hand while gesticulating with the other at his counterpart from the *Journal-Chronicle*. A couple of guys that looked to be in their eighties were talking next to the casket, their drinks resting on the closed portion. I don't think Sally would have minded that. There was even a gentleman who'd been reputed to be the head of organized crime in the city back in the early fifties that Sally had written a series of articles on, who was chatting with the former D.A. of that era.

I noticed Flannigan hovering on the edge of a group of retired Homicide Squad detectives, though from the way he was scanning the crowd, it was clear that he was interested more in spotting potential suspects than the conversation. I caught his eye and he nodded.

Janet and I ended up in a corner talking to Max Tully. Other than Cleveland and Sandage, I didn't really know most of the people there, and it turned out that Max didn't either, so it was just natural that we hung out together. It was inevitable, too, that the topic of conversation would turn to Sally's murder and that of Josh Black.

"You've got Flannigan's ear, Frank. Are the police making any progress?" Max asked.

"Not really," I responded. "They were able to get some fingerprints from both crime scenes, but they don't match anyone in the system."

"Odd, though, isn't it? In both cases it looks like the killer was known to the victim. You'd think that the police would be able to make something out of that."

If it seems a little heartless that we were talking so abstractly about the "victims" at the wake for one of them, you have to remember that our professional backgrounds made death an old acquaintance. I don't think Sally would have objected.

Lance Sinclair, the literary critic for the *Tribune-Gazette* overheard us and stopped to join the discussion. His column had highbrow pretensions, but I knew that he was a big fan of Chandler and Hammett.

"Well, what about the detective's trinity, means, motive, and opportunity?" he broke in.

"That only works in mystery novels, Lance. Real crimes aren't nearly as neat," Max answered with a laugh.

"Still, they must count for something, mustn't they?" Lance asked.

"Not so much in this case," I replied. "The means in both cases were picked spontaneously, with the killer just grabbing a weapon at hand. It's not like he used some obscure poison that could be traced. As for opportunity, somehow the killer got himself invited into the victim's apartment."

"That still leaves motive, doesn't it?" Lance asked.

"If you can figure that one out, tell the police. Unless, that is, you think the killer is just going around knocking off mystery writers," Max said.

"I can think of a few that I wouldn't mind eliminating," Lance said archly. "Mrs. Frickle, for one. Her books are so sappy and improbable. I hate it every time I have to review one."

"Don't let Flannigan overhear you," I cautioned Sinclair. It was meant as a joke, but we all looked over in the detective's direction.

"Besides, her fans adore her," Max commented. "I wish mine were as loyal."

"Oh, look, there's Harold Gaskell," Lance said, pointing to an elderly man shuffling in with a walker. He was escorted by a woman in her fifties that seemed more concerned with his balance than anything else. "I wasn't sure if he'd be able to make it. He hasn't been in good health, lately."

"Well, we can probably rule him out as the killer," Max chuckled. I'm not sure he could even have picked up that award of Josh's."

"It's too bad he stopped writing," Lance said. "He did some good work back in the forties."

"I think he came to the conclusion that he had to make a living, instead. He took a job with an ad agency," Max said. "He had a family to support. That's one of his daughters with him."

"I should go over and greet him in any case," Sinclair said.

After he left, Max exclaimed, "Oh, no. Speaking of people to eliminate—"

I followed his gaze towards the door where there was a chubby guy in his mid-forties wearing an ill-fitting suit and a tie that was too loud for a wake, even Sally's. It was Jerry Frenzel.

"What's he doing here?" I asked.

"Probably trying to push a manuscript on someone," Janet commented. She'd been quiet most of the evening, but I sensed that there was something more behind her comment than plain cattiness. Janet usually isn't malicious, but she is a good judge of people.

"I didn't know that you knew Frenzel," I said.

"He was always bothering Ezekial," Janet answered vehemently. "He was a real pest. Ezekial made the mistake once, of actually accepting one his manuscripts to read over. After that Frenzel seemed to look on him as a sort of mentor. Ezekial tried to be polite at first, but finally he lost patience. He did a full scale critique of one of Frenzel's stories. He wasn't kind, but then the story was terrible."

"What happened after that?" I asked. Janet and I rarely talked about her time with Handler. I really didn't know much about the man.

"Frenzel threw a tantrum. He said that he'd get back at Ezekial when he became famous. Of course, there was never any danger of that happening, at least not as a writer. I don't think he's ever managed to sell anything."

"He tried the same trick with me," Max said. "I read a couple of pages. That was all I could take. I sent it back with a note saying that my agent had advised me that I shouldn't read other author's material to avoid the chance of being sued for using their ideas. That seemed to shut him up, at least."

I knew from personal experience that Max was usually helpful with aspiring writers. He certainly had helped me.

"He probably just moved on to someone else," I added. "After *Murder After Midnight* was published, he sent me the manuscript for a novel. It stunk. I don't even know how he found out where my office was."

"He's been trying the same stunt for years," Max said. "I know that he had tried to push various things onto Sally and Josh Black. Nothing you could do would discourage him. Except for the lawyer trick, I mean. I have to admit, that was brilliant on my part."

"Say, you don't think he had anything to do—?"

Max interrupted me, "Naw. Frenzel is all talk. He doesn't strike me as the kind of guy who takes action."

I had to agree. Besides, there was no way that he could have been the man in the video at the Preston Arms. Even with lifts, he wouldn't have been tall enough and a trench coat wouldn't have concealed his waist line. Besides, Josh wouldn't have invited him into his study, and Sally *certainly* wouldn't have made him a drink.

We might have said more, but the time had come for the service, what there was of it. Mainly it consisted of people telling reminiscences of Sally, most of which featured corpses or whiskey, sometimes both. When the service broke up, most people stuck around for more drinks. I noticed that Frenzel was gone.

Chapter Eleven

Janet had a "girl's night out" planned with some of her charity friends, which left me to my own devices for the evening. She'd left something for me to warm up for dinner, but I decided to go out instead. Don't get me wrong, Janet's a great cook, but she tends towards the fancy and the healthy. There are times a guy just wants something greasy that's likely to give him heartburn. I didn't get much opportunity for that, so I took advantage of the situation.

There's a little corner place, Momma Rosa's, not too far from the apartment, that sells pizza by the slice. It's not a big place, just a half dozen small tables covered with checkered table cloths, but the food is good for what it is. When I got there they had a deluxe pie ready, Italian sausage, pepperoni, peppers and black olives, so I ordered a couple of slices of that and a beer to wash it down with.

I finished the first slice and got another beer to go with the second slice. Maybe it was the weather, but the place was pretty dead. The only other customers were a young couple sitting at a table next to the front door who were ignoring the pizza between them and gazing into each other's eyes. That was something that I had missed with Janet, the whole courtship phase. She'd walked into my office one morning to hire me to track down Handler's killer. It wasn't too many days after that that she was holding a smoking .45, having just saved my life by plugging Handler's murderer just before he was going to shoot me. After that, well it was intense, but not terribly romantic, not in the holding hands and longing gazes sort of way. Not that I'm complaining, but it got me to thinking, and Momma Rosa's isn't a place to think.

I've found that beer isn't the best beverage to think over, either. For that, I needed someplace smoky and some hard liquor. I got out the car and headed to the Blue Angel.

Now, you might think that the Blue Angel was an odd choice if what I wanted to do was think, but the truth is I thought that the atmosphere might provide some stimulation, while, what distractions it offered, I could ignore.

It was still early in the evening and a Wednesday, which is always a slow night, anyway, and there weren't that many people in the audience. A rookie comic had the stage, but no one seemed to be paying too much attention to him. I grabbed an empty stool at the end of the bar farthest from the stage and ordered a rye on the rocks and stared at the mirror behind the bar.

I'd been sitting there for a few minutes when Jo's form loomed up behind me. She was wearing a black sequined number with a slit up the side revealing her thigh. Personally, I preferred the red gown she'd worn the last time I'd been in, not that it matters.

"Frank? About the other night—"

The phrase was getting familiar. Max Tulley had used nearly the same words when I'd talked with him over the phone. I hadn't seen Jo since the night I'd come in to talk to the Professor, so I was a little confused.

"Which night was that, Jo?"

"It was when—" I'd never seen Jo blush before, at least not in that way.

Now I was the one confused. "When what?"

"Well, you wandered in here during my set and you got a seat at the bar. Just about where you're sitting now. After I sang "Lili Marlene" I came over to say hi. You acted like you didn't know me, but then you started flirting with me. I know you don't swing that way, or at least I thought you didn't. But it was almost as if you didn't know that I wasn't—well, a woman. I'm a little confused, Frank. And—well, a little hurt if you were just playing around with me. And if you weren't—well, then I don't know what to think."

"What night was this, Jo?" I asked, starting to get a bad feeling, like the hairs on the back of my neck were stiffening.

"It was last Thursday," Jo answered looking at me a little strangely.

"Jo, I want you to believe me. I wasn't in here on Thursday."

"Sure you were," Jo said, standing a bit straighter. I was afraid for a moment that the steelworker Joe that Jo had been was going to come out and pop me in the snout.

"Look, Jo. You've got to believe me, but it wasn't me." It was my turn to be confused again. From the look on Jo's face, she was trying to decide between being mad or feeling hurt. That's hard enough for a guy to deal with in a real woman, but with Jo—. "I'm not doubting you, Jo, but I wasn't in here that night. How sure are you that this guy was really me?"

Jo looked at me like I was crazy, but then confusion crossed her face. "I was standing as close to you as I am now. Whoever it was certainly looked like you."

"It wasn't me, Jo. Trust me." I tried to sound sincere, which isn't always easy for me, but I wanted Jo to believe me. "The thing is, I think there's a guy running around town with my face."

Jo looked like she wanted to believe me, but wasn't sure, kind of like a puppy when you pet them just after you wacked them with a newspaper. "You're serious, aren't you, Frank?" Jo replied, her voice dropping an octave.

"Deadly serious, I'm afraid. Look, this is important, Jo. I want you to tell me everything that you can remember about this guy. What he said, what he seemed to know and what he didn't."

"All right, Frank. Though you're beginning to scare me." Under any other circumstances that statement would have gotten a laugh. Jo isn't easily intimidated and she's got the physique to back it up. But I kind of understood where she was coming from. This was an odd situation, and Handler or not, there had always seemed to be a thread that bound the two of us.

"Just take it easy, Jo. One thing at a time."

"Okay, Frank. Like I said earlier, this guy that came in here was sitting at the bar. He was wearing a suit like yours, he was wearing a fedora, and there was a trench coat like yours draped over the stool. Let's face it, Frank, how many guys wear trench coats and fedoras these days?" The sarcasm in the last sentence told me that Jo and I were good again.

"Maybe some guy trying to impersonate me."

"If that's so, he was doing a pretty good job of it. He had your voice and the mannerisms down pat. His posture when he sat was exactly like yours." Jo has gotten pretty good at reading people by paying attention to the details.

"Okay. Go on. You said that he didn't seem to know you?"

"Yeah, that's right. I said hello and asked how Janet was. That seemed to draw a blank. I didn't think anything of it at the time. Well, I went on with something like 'how's it been, big boy?' You know, my usual patter that I give to all the regulars and friends. He didn't react the way you normally would. He seemed to be taking me seriously. Like I was really a woman. Frankly, it was a little creepy, Frank."

"I can imagine. So what happened next?"

"We talked for awhile. But like I said, it was like he didn't know that I'm not a woman. It was like he was interested, but didn't know what to do about it, if you know what I mean."

"I'm starting to get the idea, Jo. It was like he was trying to impersonate me but didn't know all the fine details."

"Yeah, something like that. Anyway, I was starting to get a little creeped out by it all. I wasn't sure what was going on, like whether it was just a gag or something. So I left and went backstage. When I came out later, he was gone."

"Did anyone else that knows me see this guy?"

"No, not that I know of. The Professor is the only one that really knows you by more than sight, and he was in his dressing room the whole time. You don't think I made all this up, do you, Frank?"

"The thought never crossed my mind, Jo." In fact, it hadn't. The whole incident had clearly upset Jo too much. "I was just wondering if there was anyone else that might have noticed something about this guy."

That seemed to satisfy Jo. But the implications were starting to dawn on her. "What's going on, Frank?"

"Jo, I wish I knew. As I said, it looks like there's some guy going around impersonating me. I'm not sure why, or what he's up to. The thing is, Jo, he might be dangerous. I'm serious about that. The next time you see me, make sure it's me before you get too close."

"Now you *are* scaring me, Frank," Jo said, the concern showing below her makeup.

"I'm scaring myself a little, Jo."

"But you don't know what's going on? Or is it just that you won't tell me?"

"Maybe a little bit of both, Jo. I'm starting to get an idea of what's going on, but I don't like direction it's taking me."

Jo got a look on her face like a momma bear protecting her cub, and I was the cub. I could do worse than to have Jo on my side. "Is there anything I can do, Frank? Seriously. If there's any way I can help?"

"Just be careful, Jo. And if you run into the Professor, you might ask him about *doppelgangers.*"

"Doppelgangers?" Jo said, a puzzled look on her face.

"Yeah. Doppelgangers. It's his word, not mine."

Jo must have decided she wasn't going to get any more clarity out of me, at least that night. "Look, I've gotta go, Frank. I'm up soon. Take care, and let me know if I can help."

"Sure thing, Jo."

After she headed back stage, I decided that I'd done enough thinking for the night and headed home.

Chapter Twelve

I was sitting in the office the next day, still thinking about Jo's encounter with my evil twin. That had me worried. Jo knew me a lot better than either Josh Black or Sally Johnson had. If even she could be fooled—admittedly at the bar in the Blue Angel where the lighting isn't that great—but all the same, could I count on any of my friends not being caught off guard?

I was still mulling that over when there was a knock at the door. I got up to unlock it; I had taken to locking it after I had talked to Max Tully. When I opened the door, I found the Professor standing in the hallway.

"Is this an inopportune time, Frank?" The Professor's manners and speech reflect an earlier part of the century.

"No, not at all." Actually, I was glad to see him. I felt the need to talk to someone, and the Professor seemed to be the only one I could confide in without creating complications. "I was just sitting here thinking, and not very successfully, at that."

"Well, perhaps I can help. As they say, two heads are better than one. Though, come to think of it, there was a two-headed lizard in the sideshow with a carnival with which I was associated in my youth. It didn't seem to help the poor creature at all. It never could seem to make up its mind as to which direction to turn."

I laughed at that. It struck me that it was the first time I'd laughed in days.

"Have a seat, Professor," I motioned towards one of the chairs facing the desk. "Can I offer you a drink? I'm afraid all I've got is rye."

"No, nothing for me, Frank. It's a bit early in the day."

"So, what can I do for you?" I asked after I had regained my seat behind the desk.

"Jo asked me a curious question last night after the show."

"Oh?"

"Yes. She asked me about doppelgangers. Curious, isn't it? We were just discussing the subject the other day, weren't we?"

"I'm afraid I put the notion of asking you in Jo's head," I confessed. "Did she happen to mention why she was interested?"

"You mean did she tell me about her encounter with your sinister double the other night? I assume that it *really* wasn't you?"

"Trust me, Professor, it wasn't me."

He gave a little shake of his head. "That's what I was afraid of. It would seem to indicate that this individual is an instance of something more than just someone wearing a clever disguise."

"I'm not sure I follow you, Professor," I responded. The truth was, I was afraid that I followed where he was leading all too well.

"It's easy enough to create a disguise or an illusion that will fool most people at a distance. I do it all the time on the stage. It's the cornerstone of most stage magic, after all. It happens all the time in real life, too, where you spot what you think is an acquaintance at a distance, but when you come up close you realize that the individual looks nothing like the person you took them for. It's quite another thing, though, to fool someone at close range, particularly when the people are as well acquainted with each other as are you and Jo."

"Let's face it, the Blue Angel isn't known for good lighting."

"Is that what you really believe, Frank? That Jo mistook this person for you just because the lighting was bad?"

"Well, maybe not. But there's got to be a rational explanation. What about plastic surgery, for instance?"

"Frank, I'm disappointed in you. That sort of thing only occurs in fiction, and usually not very good fiction at that. As a writer, you should know that."

"Okay. So this guy didn't have some plastic surgeon copy my mug. How do you explain it then, Professor?"

"Unfortunately, I can't. Not in rational terms, at least. But, do you remember the latter part of our conversation the other night? You must have, because of what you said to Jo."

"About doppelgangers? Yeah, I remember. But that was all just mumbo-jumbo, wasn't it?"

"At the time I thought so. I just brought it up because— well, because I am who I am, I guess. Now, though, I'm not so sure. It's unfortunate that I wasn't present during Jo's encounter."

"Why is that?"

"You may remember that I told you once that I could see auras around people."

"Yeah, I remember. You mentioned it when I gave you a ride from Mrs. DuVille's the night of the séance."

I've never been sure whether the Professor's psychic powers are legit or not. I get the impression that he's not sure himself half the time.

"Yes. I don't sense them all the time, of course, that would be disconcerting. But sometimes I do, when the circumstances are right. Particularly when I first meet someone."

"Where is this going, Professor?"

"You'll remember that I said that you're aura was distinctive. Completely unlike most people, with a few exceptions. Jo is one of them. So is that of Lt. Flannigan."

"Okay, so I've got a distinctive aura.   What's your point?"

"My point, Frank, is that it might have been instructive had I had the opportunity to observe the aura of the individual posing as you."

"In what way?" I asked, suddenly very interested.

"Two possibilities come to mind.   One is that this individual would have an aura identical to yours.   The other possibility, of course, is that it would not be a match at all."

"Okay.   Either our auras match or they don't.   I'm still not sure why that would be important."

"I see I'm not making myself clear, perhaps because my thoughts on the subject are a little fuzzy.   Let's say that the aura was a match to yours.   Then this individual would really be your *psychic* twin.   But, if this individual had an aura like that of a normal person, well, then maybe his resemblance to you has a more mundane explanation, such as clever makeup or, well—plastic surgery."

"Okay, I guess I get that. I think.   But, unfortunately you didn't see this guy, so we don't know which case is correct."

"Unfortunately, no.   I fear I misspoke, earlier.   There is a third possibility which I didn't mention."

"Which is?"

"That the aura is not an exact match but is—well, for want of a better term, a mirror image of your own."

I wasn't sure what he meant by that.   I'm not a psychic and I don't see auras.   I got the impression, that the Professor wasn't completely sure what he meant, either.

"And, what would that mean?"

"In some of the literature on doppelgangers, the double isn't an exact duplicate but is, instead, a *reflection* of the original.   Much like that which you seen in a mirror.   There's a curious story by Poe, *William Wilson*, that involves just such a phenomena.   I think I mentioned it when we talked before. I guess that what I'm saying is that if the aura was a reflection of your own, than it would support the theory that we are dealing with a true *doppelganger* and not just some sort of clever illusion."

"I see. I guess."

"I'm not sure you do, Frank. Do you know the derivation of the word *sinister*?"

"It comes from the Latin word for left, doesn't it?"

"Exactly. It's taken on the meaning of being on the left-hand or wrong side of things. Which is why doppelgangers, as reflections, are so often considered to be the evil-twin of the original."

"That would explain why this twin of mine is going around bumping off people. Though I'm not sure why he's just been picking off mystery writers."

"That is something of a puzzle, I have to admit," the Professor said.

It was a lot to wrap my head around, and the Professor left me to think in silence. Finally, I said:

"There's something that's been bugging me for a few days. Something I've been trying to recall. This talk about reflections has jogged my memory. The first time we talked about doppelgangers, you mentioned reflections, but I guess I wasn't paying attention, or at least didn't understand the implications at the time. They were able to lift some prints from the statue that was used to kill Joshua Black. They didn't match mine, which helped to clear me. The killer held the statue in his left hand. I'm right handed. But the curious thing is that the fingerprint guy said that the prints were a mirror image of the ones on my *right* hand."

"Oh, dear." The Professor shook his head in concern.

"Yeah. Oh, dear is right." That pretty much seemed to sum things up. "Are you sure you wouldn't like a drink?"

The Professor pondered my inquiry for a moment before responding. "Given the circumstances, perhaps a small one wouldn't be out of order."

I reached into the lower right hand drawer of my desk and pulled out a bottle of rye and two glasses. The glasses matched—part of a set that Janet had presented to me on the day of our wedding. It was about the only improvement she had made in my office. I think I've mentioned before that she's the perfect wife.

"Sorry, but I'm afraid I don't have any ice."

"That's quite alright. Over the years I've learned to make do without the amenities."

I poured a couple of fingers of the amber liquid into each of the glasses, sliding one across the desk towards the Professor. He took it in his hand, gazing into the glass as if it were a crystal ball before taking a sip.

I said, "Let's, for the sake of argument, accept for the moment that there are such things as doppelgangers, and that whoever, or whatever killed Josh Black and Sally Johnson is one. Just what are the implications?"

The Professor set his glass on the edge of the desk. "I'm afraid you're asking the wrong person, Frank. I'm by no means an expert in occult phenomena. I'm a stage magician, not a sorcerer or a wizard. What little I know of such matters is what I've picked up to use in the patter I spout as part of my act. For those purposes something doesn't have to be true, it just has to sound good. A little bit of voodoo, a reference to the 'mystic east,' anything to divert the attention of the marks in the audience. That's all I'm concerned with."

"But you must know more than that, Professor. Don't forget, I've seen you in action."

"That's more than I can say, if you are referring to those instances when it appears I'm acting as a channel to the spirit world. Don't forget, when I'm in a trance, I have no knowledge of what is happening, nor do I recall the events afterwards."

To tell the truth, I've never been sure about what went on during the séances I was part of with the Professor. Who better to pull a con during one than a stage magician? On the other hand, it is hard to understand how the Professor could have been privy to the information that was exchanged during those sessions without his being in touch with the recently departed. I'd just considered my experiences with spiritualism to be one of those things it didn't bear too much to think about.

"That may be true, Professor, but at the moment you are all I've got."

"Very well, but remember, what I know are just the tidbits that I've picked up from my reading over the years and talking to other carnies and magicians, most of whom were con-artists of one flavor or another. I can't vouch for the veracity of any of it."

"I'll keep that in mind. I won't hold you responsible for anything you say."

"That's very understanding of you, Frank."

The Professor was quiet for a moment as if putting his thoughts in order.

"In the first place, the lore on doppelgangers isn't very consistent on how or when they are created. In some cases, such as that described by Poe in 'William Wilson', the doppelganger is essentially a twin, someone born at the same moment as the original who then goes through life in a normal manner with various degrees of entanglement with the original until the eventual, usually fatal, confrontation."

"That's encouraging," I remarked.

"Of course, that's just in literature where the melodramatic is the whole point of the story. In some cases, the two duplicates basically live out separate but parallel lives and it's only upon some chance meeting between the two that they find they have followed the same occupation, married spouses with the same name, had the same number of children; something that sometimes is reported with identical twins separated at birth."

"What happens then?"

"Nothing, usually. They remark on the coincidence and then go their separate ways."

"So one of the twins doesn't go around murdering people?"

"No, not usually. But what shows up in books is mostly anecdotal."

"Okay. That's one kind of doppelganger. Are there others?"

"Again, what I know may be apocryphal. But another type of doppelganger is one that is created by some mystical means, a spell, a magic mirror, or some other form of sorcery. It may involve a 'glamour' by which an individual is given the appearance of someone else, or it may involve creating a new being in the image of someone, usually with the intent that the being is under the control of its creator. Somewhat analogous to the golem in Hebrew folklore, but of course, less crude in appearance."

"I'll take your word for it, Professor. If I get what you are saying, it seems more likely that what we're dealing with is the latter sort. Someone has created a replica of me to go around killing people that he wants to get rid of. Does that about sum it up?"

"That would seem to be a logical assumption. Of course, the implication of that is that magic *is* real. That's a lot to swallow, even for someone such as myself.   Especially for someone such as myself."

"I'm not so sure about that, that magic isn't real. There's something I want to show you, Professor. I've never let anyone see it, and I'd appreciate it if you would keep what you are about to see to yourself."

The Professor raised his right hand and said, "You have my word, Frank." I believed him.

I got up and went over to the safe, opened it and pulled out a sealed manila envelope marked "confidential." Back at my desk, I used a pen-knife to slit open the seal. Inside was a smaller, unsealed envelope and a letter.

"This is a letter that Ezekial Handler wrote the day he died. He left it with his lawyers with instructions to mail it to me in the event that he and Buckley, the man who murdered him, were both dead. I received it, along with a check for ten thousand dollars, about a month after the events surrounding his murder. The signature on the letter match others that I know were made by Handler. The check was good.   As to the letter—well, you'd better read it yourself."

I handed the letter over to the Professor. He pulled a pair of reading glasses out of his jacket pocket and read the letter carefully, then went back and read it again. I, of course, knew what was in the letter. I knew it by heart. In it, Handler explained that he had created me and several others, including Janet, Flannigan, Jo, and even Armand who ran the newsstand downstairs, all with the purpose of avenging his death.

"You don't really believe this, do you, my boy?"

"I don't know what to believe, Professor.   The explanation is consistent with the facts. I have to say that my recollection of my own past is pretty fuzzy. But I also know that it's a pretty incredible thing to be true. I've tried by best not to think about it. If true, the implications are—"

"I understand. But now, you think that someone else has used the same means to create a second you—"

"That's what I'm afraid of. The question is, what should I do about it? I can't very well go to the police, even Flannigan, with this story—"

"No, of course not. I'm not sure I can offer you any guidance," the Professor said regretfully. "But I can give you a cautionary warning."

"What's that, Professor?"

"In the stories, when the original and the doppelganger meet, the results are usually fatal to both of them. Sort of like what happens when matter and anti-matter meet."

"I see. And what happens to all the others? Jo, Flannigan, Janet?"

"I can't tell you that, Frank. I just don't know."

"But there is a chance they could all just go blooey, too? Just wink out of existence?"

The Professor gave a sad little shrug. "This is a matter beyond my experience, Frank."

"I was afraid you were going to say that. Thanks for your help, anyway."

"Of course. If there is any other way in which I can be of help, let me know. And, Frank. Your secret is safe with me."

Chapter Thirteen

After the Professor had gone, I went to return Handler's letter to the safe. As I did so, I noticed the key to the filing cabinet where I had hidden the late author's notebook. At the time that I had secreted it away, I had never wanted to see the damned thing again, but that had been before two people had been murdered, two people that had been my friends. If their deaths were somehow tied in with Handler, his diary might contain some clue that would reveal the killer before he killed again. How could I not examine it, regardless of the consequences for me personally?

I took the key from the safe and unlocked the file cabinet. The notebook was still in the bottom drawer where I'd placed it. Part of me had been hoping that it had disappeared in a puff of smoke, but it hadn't. I took it out and brought it over to the desk where the light was better.

Setting my typewriter to one side, I laid the book in front of me at the center of the desk where I could examine it under the illumination of my desk lamp. It wasn't overly large, roughly ten inches tall, eight inches wide and about an inch and a quarter thick. The covering was a dark leather, almost black in color. There was a faint tracery of scales in the leather as if it had come from something reptilian. A stout strap wrapped around the middle, closed by a clasp and lock.

On the cover, there was some faint lettering in an ink a shade darker than the leather itself, but try as I could, I couldn't make out what it said. I tried tilting the book at various angles under the light of the desk lamp, but the inscription remained indecipherable. All I could tell for certain was that the letters did not belong to the Roman alphabet, at least as I knew it.

I paused for a moment, uncertain whether I wanted to continue. Handler, in the last months of his life had become obsessed with magic, not the stage sort as practiced by the Professor, but the real deal, or at least what he believed was real. He had amassed a vast collection of grimoires, spell-books, and alchemical apparatus, and from what I had discovered during the investigation of his death, he had been conducting arcane experiments. Janet, who at the time had lived in a separate apartment, the same one where we lived now, knew little about that part of Handler's life or the nature of these experiments, and had been reluctant to talk about them. For my part, I hadn't had any desire to pursue the subject. Not knowing what the notebook contained, did I really want to open it when it might prove to be a literal Pandora's Box?

I decided that, having come this far, I had to proceed. However, practical difficulties stood in my way in the form of the stout strap wrapped around the middle, closed by a clasp and lock. The lock didn't look like the ordinary cheap affair, the kind that can be picked with a bent paperclip. It was much more intricate in appearance, and more substantial. I thought for a moment of just cutting the strap, but some premonition prevented me from doing so; a feeling that if I did sever the strap, the contents of the diary might be destroyed or something worse might happen.

I pulled out a small, flat case from the top drawer of the desk. Technically, possession of such a case, or at least its contents, was a violation of the law, but the reality is that most private investigators keep some sort of collection of lock picks and other burglary tools. Frank Slade, P.I. had been no exception. I unzipped the case and laid it flat next to the book. I might as well not have bothered. Though I probed the keyhole for over a quarter of an hour, the lock refused to yield. I would need the key to open the notebook.

When Janet and I had cleaned out Handler's mansion, we had dumped the contents of his desk into a shoebox. The shoebox had ended up with all his personal papers, the papers that filled the banker's boxes that were currently stacked in my office. I started opening boxes, searching for it. It goes without saying that I found the shoebox in the last one I opened.

I took it back to the desk and lifted the lid. Inside was the usual clutter that collects in a desk, pens, pencil stubs, paperclips and rubber bands. Like most people, Handler had also collected a random assortment of keys, keys to doors of former residences, keys to pieces of luggage, the key to the case of his typewriter, keys to who knows what, all of which had lain unlabeled in the drawers of his desk. Most of them were the wrong size or shape. Those that would fit, I inserted in the lock, but none of them would open the clasp.

I was getting frustrated, and was about ready to stuff the diary back into the file cabinet when it occurred to me that I had my own accumulation of keys. I had no reason to think that any of them would fit the lock, but I wouldn't know that until I tried. I opened the center drawer of the desk, where I stashed my own personal clutter. The keys mostly had gotten shoved toward the back in the normal course of events. I reached in and pulled out a handful of junk. Separating the keys from the paperclips, bottle openers and bits of string, I examined them, looking for one that might fit the lock. None of them were of any more use than Handler's had been. One last time I stuck my hand into the drawer, feeling into the back corners where I couldn't see. My fingers felt a flat bit of metal, wedged between the drawer bottom and the back of the drawer.

It took a bit of effort to free the object, but when I finally was able to examine it, it was indeed a key. On the surface, there was nothing special about it, just a flat piece of some metal. It was maybe a little thicker than most, but it had the usual flat handle on one end and the shaft on the other end, though the teeth that had been cut into it looked a little more intricate than those usually found on such keys.

As I inspected the key under the light of the desk lamp, it occurred to me that I had no recollection of where I had acquired it or what lock it was supposed to fit. The metal might have been steel, or it might not. When I held it so that the lamp's light raked the surface, I could see that faint lines had been etched into the surface on one side, lines that might have formed those angular characters known as runic, but which might as well just have been random scratchings.

Having come this far, I inserted the key in the lock on the book. It seemed to fit with a snugness that none of the other keys I had tried had exhibited. I tried to turn the key clockwise, but was met with firm resistance, but when I turned it in the opposite direction, there was a sharp "snick" from the lock. I tried tugging on the strap and discovered that it now slid free.

For a moment, I thought about getting the bottle of rye from the desk and having a quick shot to bolster my courage, but decided against doing so. Instead, I opened the book.

I quickly discovered that it was upside down. Contrary to normal practice, the binding was on the right hand side, not the left. I supposed that Handler had some mystical reason for this, and for a moment I wondered if the writing would be a mirror image as in the notebooks of Leonardo. This was not the case. Instead, when I had turned the book around and opened it to the title page I saw the single word

"BEHOLD" along with Handler's name and a date about six months before his death. It occurred to me that the book might be nothing more than a hoax or practical joke on the part of the author.

I leafed through the first few pages which were covered in inscriptions in Latin, Greek, and what I thought was Hebrew. Interspersed with these bits of text were odd symbols, some of which I recognized as representing the planets or chemical elements. Others bore a resemblance to those that I had seen thumbing through a book of Handler's about the Elizabethan mathematician and sorcerer, John Dee. I couldn't even begin to decipher the meaning of what I saw.

As I flipped further through the book, I came across a page in English. At the top was a date and a name, "Armand O'Hara." Armand O'Hara, at least the one I knew was an ex-jockey that ran the newspaper stand in the lobby on the ground floor. Below the name was a detailed description, not only of Armand's appearance, but of his history, background, and mannerisms.

I'd been through enough of notebooks that Handler's had created for his novels to know that they typically would include a list of characters and thumbnail descriptions of each. It was a common and useful enough practice, one that I had adopted for *Death Buys a Condo,* but this description was much more detailed than what Handler had typically included in those notebooks.

The next page was dated the next day and had a curious entry:

It appears the attempt has been successful. At least when I went to the lobby of the office building, there was a newsstand in the lobby. I engaged the operator in conversation and learned that his name actually was Armand O'Hara. It is, of course, possible that this is all a coincidence. I will have to conduct further experiments to be sure, but it seems my plan may be feasible.

A chill ran up the back of my neck. In Handler's last letter, he had described Armand as the first of the characters that he had created in his plan to exact vengeance on Buckley, a sort of trial run or "proof of concept." Was I reading evidence that Handler had actually conducted such an experiment?

I flipped the page. The date was two days later, the heading was "Lt. Flannigan," and below that was another detailed description. The notes on the following page indicated success and included some suggestion for refining the procedure.

The name on the next page was The Blue Angel, and the description included not only details of the club, but a sketch of its floor plan. The notation as to the results of the experiment read:

It seems that I am able to create not only people, but locations. What the practical application of this is, I am uncertain, but I shall keep it in mind. I must begin to work out the details of the plot.

I wasn't surprised when the name on the following page was Joseph Jaworski, with Josephine LaTouche in parentheses. The description matched that of the female impersonator. There was also a précis of what role Jo would play in the plot to catch Buckley, one that followed the actual events quite closely. The date on the page was five weeks before Handler had been murdered.

I was afraid to read further, but found that I could not avoid turning the pages of the notebook. It was inevitable what the next heading would be. It read, simply, "Janet Nielsen."

I slammed the book shut and stuck the strap through the clasp. My heart was pounding and a cold sweat was breaking out on my forehead. Reading Handler's last letter had been one thing, to find evidence that he had actually carried out the sorcerous experiments that he had claimed to, experiments which were responsible for creating my closest friends, was something else, entirely. That Janet, my beloved wife, was nothing more than a puppet created as part of a mad scheme of vengeance and retribution—

The ultimate implication, of course, was that I was a construct as well, a golem, a puppet, a *thing*.

But, how could I be certain that the notebook was actually what it appeared to be? How could I be certain that Handler had even written it? The handwriting had looked to be Handler's, but I was no expert on such matters, and handwriting can be forged. Was it possible the journal was a hoax? Had it been created after the fact? But, if so, for what purpose? To drive me mad? To create a wedge between me and my friends? Was it an act of revenge? If so, by whom?

I knew I had no immediate answers to any of these questions. There might be scientific tests that could verify the date or authenticity of the journal, but did I want to risk the answers they might give? Did I want to risk my existence?

I replaced the journal in the bottom drawer of the filing cabinet, and locked the key to the cabinet in the safe. The key to the journal I clipped to the key-chain in my pocket.

Chapter Fourteen

The next day I stopped at the newsstand in the lobby on the way to my office to pick up the morning *Tribune-Gazette*. I'd known the guy who ran the stand as long as I could remember, though I was no longer certain as to just how long that was.

As I waited to pay Armand, I found myself comparing him to Handler's description in the notebook:

Armand O'Hara: Short, slight of build and vaguely Hispanic, most likely of Puerto Rican descent. Former jockey. Walks with a slight limp due to a racing accident in which a horse fell on his right leg. Speaks fluent English but with a noticeable accent. Operates the newsstand in the lobby of the office building at 917 Oak Street. Friendly and outgoing, especially to regular customers. Always knows the details behind the stories in the latest headlines. Very observant and more intelligent than most people give him credit for.

Needless to say, the description was a match to the reality. The question was, was that because it was a detailed observation on the part of Handler, or was it, as the notebook claimed, a design specification? I didn't have an answer.

"Hey, Mr. Slade," Armand said, as I handed over a buck, "You working on a new case? I thought you geeve up on the P.I. beesness."

"Why are you asking, Armand?"

"When you went up last night you deedn't say hello."

"Sorry about that," I apologized. I'd always been on friendly terms with Armand. He was a nice guy, always friendly and outgoing, but he also was a useful source of information. He actually read the papers that he sold and had a habit of keeping his ears open.

"You seemed pretty distracted. Not your usual self. That's why I thought maybe you were on a case."

"What time was this?"

"Oh, I don't know. Maybe seven, seven-thirty. A leetle beet before I close up."

"I guess I must have been distracted, Armand. Not that I'm on a case. But with these murders—well, I knew both of them."

"Yes, Joshua Black and the woman meestery writer, Sally Johnson. Eets too bad. Say, you don't think that this keeler is going after meestery writers, do you Mr. Slade? That might mean you could be next."

"I don't know about that, Armand. The police aren't sure what the motive is yet, but it's a possibility. Look, Armand, if you see anything suspicious happening around the building, why don't you let me know. Pronto. I'll make it worth your while."

"Sure thing, Mr. Slade."

"Thanks for the paper. Keep the change. And Armand?"

"Si?"

"Be careful. Make sure you know who you're dealing with." I didn't add that the person he should be looking out for looked a lot like me.

Armand nodded, looking a little confused, but then his normal smile returned to his face.

As I rode up in the elevator I mulled over what Armand had said. I'd left the building about five-thirty in the afternoon and hadn't come back. At seven I was having dinner in the apartment with Janet. Was it merely a case of mistaken identity? Armand knew me pretty well, but if he had only seen the person from the back—men in trench coats and fedoras look pretty much the same from that angle. Still, most of the other tenants didn't normally work late and the building usually wasn't very busy in the evening.

I began to get worried as to what Armand's stranger might have been up to. Had he been looking for me, perhaps with the intention of adding me to the list of victims? Or, and this was of more concern, had he been interested in something else, perhaps something in my office? Something like Handler's notebook?

I paused at the door to my office. There were no signs of a forced entry, but the lock wouldn't have presented much difficulty to anyone with a little skill. I'd never bothered to have a better lock put in; anyone who really wanted to get in could just break the frosted glass panel that made up the upper part of the door. The brass of the door handle and escutcheon around the lock were polished bright, more through decades of wear than the efforts of the cleaning staff. If there were any fresh scratches indicating the lock had been picked, I couldn't spot them.

I inserted my key in the lock and opened the door cautiously. The office was empty. Had I let Armand's comments spook me? I couldn't tell if anything on the desk had been disturbed, but then I'd never been one of those orderly people who line everything up in nice, neat rows. As far as I could tell, nothing was missing.

I hung my hat and trench coat on the hat rack in the corner and went to check the safe. If I were one of those detectives that occupy the space between the covers of a book, I would have done something clever like spin the dial of the safe to a specific number to make it easy to detect if it had been monkeyed with. That kind of detective would probably have stuffed a matchbook between the door and the jamb to see if it had been opened in his absence. Hell, he'd probably have done half a dozen other clever things. The problem was, I wasn't that kind of detective and I hadn't done any of those things. I dialed the combination and opened the safe.

Again, nothing was missing, but I couldn't be confident that the contents hadn't been disturbed. Handler's letter was still there, at the bottom of a pile of documents. I pulled it out and inspected it. That's when I noticed it. The folded sheets of paper that comprised the letter had been inserted in the envelope in such a manner that the bottom fold of the last sheet was on the outside. I was certain that when I had put it back after showing it to the Professor that all of the sheets had been on the inside. Apparently, someone had opened my safe and examined the letter.

In a panic, I looked inside the safe for the key to the filing cabinet. To my relief, it was still there, but that didn't necessarily mean that it hadn't been used and then returned to the safe. I grabbed it and unlocked the cabinet. The notebook was still there, resting at the bottom of the drawer. The strap was still in place and the clasp was locked. Somehow, I was confident that if the lock had been forced, there would be evidence of the fact. The notebook would not have given up its secrets without a struggle.

I relocked the filing cabinet, put the key back in the safe and closed the door. As an added precaution, I spun the dial several times and then set it to precisely line up the mark with 19 on the dial.

I walked over to my desk and sat down. After a moment, I opened the right hand drawer and pulled out the bottle of rye and a glass. I felt I deserved a belt. I needed it.

I poured two fingers in the glass, put the cap back on the bottle and replaced it in the drawer. After the first long sip, I reviewed what I knew.

Someone had been gotten into my office. The chances were that someone had looked like me. The intruder had unlocked the office door, admittedly not a particularly impossible feat. They had then managed to open the door of the safe. The safe was an older one, but it dated to an age when people hadn't trusted banks with their money. I was pretty sure that to open it the intruder either had to have been an expert cracksman or had known the combination. The purpose of the break-in had been a search for information rather than money or other valuables. The information sought was related to Handler and not any of my other previous clients.

The inescapable conclusion was that somehow the break-in had something to do with the murders of Josh and Sally. Knowing that, what should I do about it?

I decided to call Flannigan. The whole doppelganger business wasn't something that I had felt comfortable discussing with the detective before. Flannigan wasn't the kind of guy to be comfortable with the mystical. A break-in, though, was something tangible, something much more up his line.

"What's up, Frank," Flannigan asked, once I got through to him. "You got something for me?"

"Maybe. I had a break-in at the office. Sometime last night."

"Anything taken?"

"Not so far as I can see, but some of my personal papers were gone through."

"Burglary really isn't my line, Frank. In case you've forgotten, I've got two unsolved homicides on my hand. I can transfer you over to Property Crimes if you want."

"The thing is, Flannigan, the break-in might have something to do with your murders. Armand, that's the guy who owns the newsstand in the lobby, well he saw a man in a trench coat and fedora around seven o'clock. He thought it was me, but it wasn't. I was having dinner with Janet at the time."

The "trench coat and fedora" got Flannigan's attention.

"Interesting. What do you want me to do, Frank?"

"I thought you might want to send a crime scene team over here. Take prints and whatever else they can do. I'm afraid I already messed things up seeing if anything had been taken, but it might still be worth a shot."

"At this point, I'll take anything, Frank. I'll send the fingerprint boys over right away. Hell, I'll be over there myself as soon as I can get things arranged."

"I'll be waiting." I hung up the phone and leaned back in my chair.

Chapter Fifteen

Flannigan was as good as his word. He was at my office in twenty minutes. The fingerprint team showed up five minutes later. Flannigan and I stood out in the corridor while the forensic boys took care of their business. The photographer who has an office down the hall poked his head out but a dirty look from Flannigan sent him back into hiding.

"So, Frank. Tell me what you can. Why do you think you were burgled and why do you think it was our killer?"

"There was a letter that I kept in the safe. I'd showed it to someone, Professor Longwell actually, yesterday afternoon. After he left, I stuffed it back in the envelope. When I checked up on it, it noticed that it had been taken out and when it was put back, the burglar left part of one sheet sticking out of the envelope."

"The safe had been locked?"

"Of course."

"But it wasn't broken into?"

"No, whoever opened it either knew the combination or really knew what he was doing when it comes to cracking safes."

"And this happened last night?"

"Like I said, I showed the letter to the Professor yesterday afternoon. I left the office around five or so, and I didn't come back until this morning."

"But you said that Armand saw someone in the lobby a little after seven. Someone that he thought looked like you. Is that right?"

"You can ask him yourself, but that's right. He said he saw someone that looked like me wearing a trench coat and fedora."

"But it wasn't you?"

"No. Like I said, I was at home having dinner with Janet. You can ask her if you don't believe me." I was getting a little hot being on the wrong end of Flannigan's third degree. "And no, to answer your next question, I'm not in the habit of sleep walking, and besides, I didn't go to bed until eleven. You can check with Janet on that as well, Flannigan."

"Don't take it personal, Frank. I'm just doing my job. I just want to get things straight in my head. Any chance that someone else in the building saw this guy?"

"I doubt it. Most of the other tenants don't work that late. Armand is usually the last one out and the super locks the front doors around eight."

"Too bad. All we know for sure is that your twin was down in the lobby." Flannigan wrote something down in his notebook. "If you don't mind telling me, Frank, just what was the nature of this letter. The one that you showed Longwell."

"It was a letter from Ezekial Handler."

Flannigan looked up sharply, his pencil poised in mid air.

"Handler? Just who was this letter to? That is if you can tell me."

"It was addressed to me."

"But I thought that you'd never met the man."

"I never did. He left the letter with his lawyers with instructions to post it in the event that his killer and been found and brought to justice. I received it a few weeks after his death."

Flannigan pushed his hat back on his forehead and shook his head. I wasn't surprised. I'd never gone into all the details of the Handler case with him, in particular the trail of clues that Handler had left me to solve his murder.

"Are you saying that Handler not only knew that he was going to be murdered, but that before he was killed, he wrote a letter to some guy he didn't know and left instructions to his lawyers to mail this letter after his death?"

"Yeah. That's pretty much it, Flannigan."

"And what was in the letter?"

"It was basically a thank you letter for solving his murder."

Flannigan shoved his hat back on his broad forehead. "Jeezus, Frank. I can't put something like that in my report."

"Why don't you just say it was a personal communication?"

"Yeah. I'll do that," Flannigan said sarcastically. Before we could discuss the matter further, the fingerprint guy came out to report to Flannigan.

"Find anything?" the lieutenant asked.

"You should clean your office more often, Mr. Slade," the print guy said. "It looks like it's been a while since anything has been wiped off."

"I'll mention that to the cleaning lady. I think she's due about next April."

"I found plenty of prints, mostly yours. I did manage to pull a couple of useful ones off the handle of the safe. Good thing that the guy who broke in was a lefty. That meant he grabbed the handle in a different place than you did. That's the only reason I was able to get a clean print. A thumb and forefinger."

"That's good," Flannigan said. "Let me know if you can match them with anyone in the system."

"I'll try, but I don't think I'll have much luck. But I brought along photos of the prints that we took at the Black scene. The ones on the murder weapon. They're a match."

"Thanks. That's a break. Let me have your report as soon as possible."

"I'll do that, lieutenant. Unless there's anything else you want us to look at we're pretty much done here."

"No, I think I've got what I need. The rest of the building has probably seen so many people that it wouldn't be worth much even if you did find another print."

After the fingerprint team had packed up and left, Flannigan and I went back into the office and sat down. I pulled out the bottle of rye, but Flannigan shook his head. I left the bottle on the desk in case he changed his mind.

"Looks like you were right, Frank. The killer was here, all right. You think he was after this letter? The one Handler sent you from beyond the grave?" Flannigan might have meant it as a joke, but it had never been funny.

"No. I actually think he was after something else."

"And just what was that, Frank?"

"A notebook. One that Handler was keeping in the months before he died."

Flannigan looked around at the banker's boxes. "Looks like our thief could have had his choice."

"Not those. Those are just the notebooks he kept for his writing. I don't think the killer was interested in any of those."

Flannigan raised a bushy eyebrow. "So what was in this other notebook, Frank? I take it wasn't in the safe?"

"No. I had it hidden, locked up in the filing cabinet."

Flannigan looked over at the cabinet.

"Okay. I give. What is so special about this particular notebook?"

"I'm not sure I can tell you, Flannigan. I'm not sure that you'd believe me even if I did tell you. I'm not sure I believe it, myself."

"Can we quit playing games, Frank? I've got two unsolved murders on my hand and I'm trying to prevent it from being three. And that means keeping you from maybe being the next victim. I need some help here, Frank."

I thought it over a minute. In his own way, Flannigan was right. He deserved to know at least part of it. The part that sort of made sense.

"Alright, but some of this is going to sound pretty far out there."

"I'll try to keep an open mind, Frank."

"The last year or so, before he died, Handler had become obsessed with the occult and the supernatural. You can see the influences in his last novel, *The Uncorrupted Corpse.* I'm not sure which came first, whether his interest in the occult resulted in that book, or whether he became interested in the subject in the process of writing it. In either case, he had gotten heavily into magic. He bought a lot of old books on the subject."

"We're not talking stage magic here, the kind your carney friend does, are we, Frank?"

"No, we're talking the real deal. Magic, sorcery, alchemy, spells and potions. The whole shebang."

"You don't really believe in any of that shit, do you Frank?"

That was a question that I didn't want to answer, not even to myself. I'd seen enough things that I didn't have a real good explanation for not to be comfortable denying possibilities.

"It doesn't really matter what you or I believe, Flannigan. Handler believed in it. He believed in it enough that he actually was performing experiments. The notebook was his record of those attempts."

"So this killer, the one that looks like you, he's after this notebook? That's what you think, isn't it, Frank?"

"That's the only thing I can see that was worth breaking in for."

Flannigan shook his head. "This is all screwy, Frank. What's so valuable about a notebook full of the delusions of a man who was going around the bend? And how do the murders tie in with it all? It just doesn't make sense."

"I admit that it's pretty crazy, Flannigan. Look, I haven't really had a chance to look through the notebook yet." I didn't mention that I had been afraid to. "The way I figure it, maybe there is something incriminating in the notebook, something that will reveal the identity of the killer, and that's why he was after it."

"That, at least, makes sense. Maybe I should take this notebook and have some of my people go over it."

"I don't think that would be such a good idea, Flannigan. What little I've read in there is pretty weird. I'm not sure that anyone who wasn't familiar with Handler and the way he was thinking would be able to get anything out of it." I didn't add that there were things within the notebook that I didn't want to get out. Things that I wasn't sure that Flannigan would be ready to deal with.

"It's evidence, Frank."

"Is it? What grounds do you have to tie it into the murders? A fingerprint on a safe that didn't even contain the notebook? Besides, the notebook belongs to me, or at least to Janet as heir to his literary estate. I'm not going to let it out of my possession without a fight."

Flannigan's Irish temper was up, and for a moment I thought he was going to fight me just for the sake of a fight, but then he backed down.

"All right. I'll let that go for the time being. But you let me know if you find anything in that damned book. You understand, Frank?"

"Don't worry, I will."

Flannigan sat there glaring at me, but then he cooled off.

"I think maybe I'll take that drink now, Frank."

I pulled out a pair of glasses and poured some of the rye into each.

"Just what the hell is going on, Frank?" Flannigan said after he had a sip. "What's the link tying everything together? It's not just the fact that Black and Johnson were mystery writers. There's something more, isn't it?"

"Yeah, I think so; I'm just not sure what. But I think it has something to do with Handler. Something that he did, something that he had found out, something that he knew. In a way, I think that the murders of Josh Black and Sally Johnson were just peripheral to what's really going on, but I haven't a clue as to why they had to die. Maybe there's something in the notebook, maybe not, but I'd bet my soul that it's got some part to play."

Flannigan looked up at me. He didn't always act it, but at heart, he was a good Catholic and he took things like the soul seriously. Me, I'm not so sure, but I knew that my existence was on the line. My existence and that of all those close to me.

"So what do you suggest we do next, Frank?"

"Maybe we should start to think like cops, Flannigan. It looks like the killer wants the notebook. He tried to get it and he failed. Maybe he'll try again. And maybe we should be waiting for him when he does."

"Just what do you have in mind?"

"A stakeout. We stakeout my office tonight, and see if he comes back for another crack at the notebook. Maybe he won't show, but maybe he will."

"Finally, something you've said makes sense."

Chapter Sixteen

After that, Flannigan and I made plans. We had to be prepared for the fact that my double might come back that night, which didn't give us much time to get ready. In the end, we kept it simple; Flannigan and I would wait in my office while an unmarked car with two detectives from the Homicide Squad would be positioned in the street below where they could keep a watch on the lobby entrance. Flannigan's instructions for the men in the car were that they weren't to interfere with anyone entering the building, but if they saw the suspect come out, they were to try and follow him. The description they were given was intentionally vague, a man of medium height and build "known to wear a trench coat and fedora."

The arrangement was that Flannigan would meet me in my office around six. That was early enough to let him blend in with the normal building traffic in case the killer was keeping an eye on the place.

I had an early dinner at home, before going back to the office. Janet wasn't particularly happy with the idea of my being on a stakeout, even though I pointed out I'd be protected by Flannigan and the two men maintaining surveillance outside. That didn't stop her from making me a thermos of hot coffee and a couple of sandwiches.

It was around five-thirty when I got back to the office. Armand was surprised to see me coming in, but I gave him a wave to let him know it was me. I had a sudden flash of inspiration, and went over to the newsstand.

"Armand, I guess you probably have heard that my office was broken into last night."

"Si, Mr. Slade."

"Well, Lt. Flannigan and I are going to be waiting up in my office tonight, just in case he comes back. The thing is, we think this guy is trying to disguise himself to look like me by wearing a hat and coat like the ones I do."

"You mean the man I saw last night—"

"Yeah, that wasn't me. Anyway, I'm going up to my office now. If you see anyone who kind of looks like me going up later, I want you to call up to the office. Can you do that?"

"Sure theeng, Mr. Slade. You can count on me."

"I knew I could, Armand. But I want you to be careful. We think this guy might be dangerous, so don't take any risks, understand? I wouldn't want anything to happen to my favorite newsie."

"Si. I'll be careful."

"Good. Flannigan will probably be coming in soon. Just ignore him."

"No problem, Mr. Slade."

Frankly, I hoped that Armand would take the hint and close up shop and go home before the killer showed up. Unfortunately, he'd probably stick around out of a sense of duty.

Up in my office, I set the coffee and sandwiches on the desk and hung up my trench coat and hat. After that, there was something I had to attend to. Even when I'd been a working P.I. I had rarely carried a firearm. You introduce a gun into a situation and too many bad things can happen. But that didn't mean I didn't know how to use one if I had to.

I had a .38 automatic in the safe. I opened the safe to get it out, noting with satisfaction that the dial had still been set on 19. As I withdrew the pistol, the key to the filing cabinet caught my eye. I didn't want to take any chances. I grabbed the key and relocked the safe door, this time setting the dial on 23.

I checked the filing cabinet to make sure that the notebook was still in place. It was. Relocking the cabinet, I looked around for a safe place to stash the key. Janet, in a misplaced effort to brighten up my office had brought in a plant. The plant had died, but I hadn't bothered to get rid of the pot which was still sitting on the window ledge. When I pulled on the dead stem, the dirt came out in a chunk. I stashed the key in the pot and replaced the remains of the plant on top of it. Not particularly original, I have to admit, but as good a temporary hiding place as any.

That taken care of, I slipped on the shoulder holster that I had hanging on the coat rack. As I said, I never used guns much, but the sight of a holster hanging from a hat tree had convinced more than one client that I was the real hard-boiled deal.

I had ejected the clip of the automatic and was checking the action of the pistol when Flannigan showed up.

"What's that for?" he asked.

"Just in case."

"You know which end the bullets come out of, Frank?"

"I'm not that far from still being a P.I., Flannigan. I've still got my license and permit."

"Well, let's hope it doesn't come to that."

"That would be fine by me. You might as well have a seat and make yourself comfortable. We've probably got a long night ahead of us."

"I hope that's coffee in the thermos," Flannigan commented after he had parked his rear in a chair.

"Janet brewed up a pot special, strong and black. She made a couple of sandwiches, too. Pastrami and Swiss on rye with a little bit of creamy coleslaw."

"You've got it made, Frank. I wish my wife would make me sandwiches like that. I'm lucky to get baloney and mayo on Wonderbread."

"That's one of the reasons I married her."

"I can think of plenty of reasons to marry a woman like Janet. What I've never figured out is why she married a two-bit P.I. like you."

"I guess it's one of those things that was just preordained." I didn't bother to tell him just how much I wasn't kidding. "We'd better turn out the lights and act like shadows."

The office wasn't really dark with the lights out. There was enough to see with, but plenty of deep shadows, too. There was some light coming in the front window from the street below and light from the hallway made it in through the frosted glass of the door and the open transom.

It wasn't particularly silent, either. Old buildings are never really quiet. We could hear the sound of doors closing, the echo of footsteps, and the noise of the elevator as one by one the other tenants left for the day. Finally, those noises subsided, but there were still the creaks and groans of the building's structure and the clanks and hissing of the steam heat in the radiators. We could hear the street noises coming in through the window, too. Oak Street was a fairly busy thoroughfare, and there was still plenty of traffic early in the evening.

Sitting in the dark, it's easy to imagine things, particularly when you're waiting for a killer to show up. I could sense that Flannigan was a little tense. I know I was. Seven came and went, then seven-thirty. I fished around in the bottom desk drawer for a couple of coffee cups and poured some out from the thermos. There was no cream or sugar, but you learn to live without on a stakeout.

I was about to break out the sandwiches when I heard the whir of the elevator motor. Strangely, it seemed to be coming from above. The thought came to me that maybe the killer had come in earlier and been hiding someplace on one of the upper floors. Old buildings like the one we were in offer plenty of nooks and crannies for someone to hide. Flannigan had heard it, too, because I saw him reach for his revolver.

Earlier, I had repositioned my desk lamp so that it was pointed at the office door. My hand reached out to the switch, ready to turn it on. The elevator stopped, and we could hear the sound of the doors opening. The faint sound of footsteps on the hall tiles echoed as the intruder approached.

We could see the silhouette of a fedora wearing figure in the frosted glass of the door backlit by the light hanging from the hallway ceiling. I couldn't tell whether or not he was wearing a trench coat because the door cut off the lower part of his torso.

The right hand of the figure moved towards the lock, and I could hear the sound of a key being inserted in the door. The bolt drew back and the door slowly swung open. As I got ready to turn on the lamp, I noticed that the intruder was holding a pistol in his left hand.

"Hold it right there," Flannigan called.

I flipped on the desk lamp and the light caught the intruder full in the face, a face that was mine. For an instant he seemed stunned, then he raised the gun and fired, aiming at nothing in particular.

I did what any red-blooded, hard-boiled private-eye would have done, I ducked behind the desk. Flannigan was a little more decisive, and tried to get out of his chair. I expected to hear the blast of another shot, but instead, I heard footsteps, louder now, as the intruder fled.

"After him, Frank," Flannigan ordered.

I got up, pulled out my automatic and followed the lieutenant out into the hallway.

"He's going for the stairs," I said.

"I'll follow him. You take the elevator and see if you can cut him off in the lobby."

I ran towards the elevator, pressed the buttons for the door and the lobby. I didn't have much hope of beating the intruder down. The elevator was an old one and anything but an express.

I fumed as it made its slow descent. Fortunately, I didn't hear the sound of another round being fired. The indicator lights for the second, and then the first floor lit. Finally, I came to the lobby, just in time to hear Flannigan's flat feet pounding down the stairs. A figure in a trench coat and fedora was just pushing his way out the lobby's front door.

Flannigan and I spilled out onto the sidewalk, looking up and down the street. The intruder was running off to the left and the two of us started after. At the corner, he turned. Behind us I heard the sound of spinning tires as the unmarked car set off in pursuit. Unfortunately, they had been pointed the wrong way, and it took a moment for them to turn around.

As we got to the corner, I heard a car door slam and then the sound of an engine starting. There were more screeching tires noises as the car sped off. The police car rounded the corner, with a red light flashing on the dash and the siren blaring. Flannigan and I watched them disappear down the road as we stopped and tried to catch our breath.

"Damn, Frank. He got away," Flannigan swore.

"Maybe the car will catch up with him," I consoled him. I wasn't too sure of that. The lead had been too much.

We stood there on the corner panting. Eventually, we remembered to holster our guns.

A few minutes later, the unmarked car returned. The two officers got out to make their report. When they saw me, their jaws dropped.

The one who had been driving finally composed himself enough to comment, "I'd swear, the guy looked just like you."

"Yeah, I've been getting that a lot lately," I replied.

"What is he, your twin brother?" the other plainclothesman asked.

"Something like that. It's complicated." I could see neither of them were really buying it.

"Sorry, Lieutenant. I'm afraid he got away," the detective that had been driving said.

"I managed to get the license number, though," the other one added. "And the make. It was a '66 Fairlane. Some dark color, blue or black, I think. Maybe dark green."

"Run a license check. Maybe we'll get lucky and it won't be stolen."

The driver of the car got in and contacted the dispatch on the radio. Meanwhile, his partner just stood there staring at me. Finally, Flannigan got annoyed and told him to stop gawking.

It took a few minutes, but the driver finally came back.

"The registration on the car is for a Ruth Frenzel, Lieutenant. The only problem is that it appears that Mrs. Frenzel is dead. She died a little over six months ago according to the dispatcher."

"Great. I'm pretty sure that wasn't any dead woman that took a shot at us," Flannigan complained.

"You want us to hang around, Lieutenant?"

"Nah. You might as well go on home. I doubt if our intruder will be back tonight."

"Maybe it's not so bad, Flannigan," I said. "I may have an idea of who's behind this business."

Flannigan looked at me. "That name mean something to you, Frank?"

"Yeah. Maybe. At least I know a Frenzel."

Chapter Seventeen

"Let's go back to my office. I've got a fresh bottle of rye and we can talk about it."

Flannigan responded with, "Suits me."

We walked back to the lobby entrance, but the door was locked. Looking through the glass, I spotted Mrs. Poldowski mopping the floor inside and pounded on the glass. Mrs. Poldowski's husband had been a captain in the Polish army until the Soviets had executed him and a few thousand of his compatriots in a forest in eastern Poland on the off chance that they might want their country back after the war. Mrs. Poldowski had managed to escape the Iron Curtain and now cleaned a run-down office building at nights to survive.

She tried to ignore me, but I can be hard to ignore. Finally she gave up and came over and shouted through the glass, "Building closed. Come back in morning."

"Anna, it's me, Frank Slade. Third floor. I want to discuss something with my friend here, detective Lt. Flannigan, up in my office. Please let us in."

Mrs. Poldowski seemed uncertain, but when Flannigan flashed his badge, that seemed to convince her. She unlocked the door and opened it, making a big show of looking up and down the street in case someone should spot her transgression.

"You know I'm not supposed to let anyone in after hours, Mr. Slade?"

"I won't tell anyone if you won't, Anna. And I'm sure that we can trust the lieutenant's discretion."

She let us in, locking the door behind us, before returning to her mop and bucket. Flannigan and I walked over to the elevator and rode it up to the third floor.

Everything was just as we'd left it, the door open, the desk lamp on and pointing at the door, Flannigan's chair tipped over from when he'd gotten up. I closed the door, turned on the overhead light, and righted the chair. While I was doing that, Flannigan had gone over to the outside wall and was probing around with a pen knife.

"Got it," he said, after extracting the slug. "Looks like a .38." He leaned down so that his head was level with the hole the slug had made in the plaster and stared towards the doorway. "Looks like it went right between our heads. A foot either way and we wouldn't be having a conversation. Probably couldn't decide which one of us to plug."

"That's comforting."

"You got an envelope I can stick this in?" Flannigan asked.

I pulled one out of the desk and handed it to Flannigan. While he was sealing the slug in the envelope, I pulled out the bottle of rye and a brace of glasses.

"Say when."

"That's enough for me," Flannigan said after I had poured a couple of fingers worth. I slid the glass across the desk top and then poured a similar amount in mine.

"You've got the ballistics for my automatic on file, don't you?" I asked as Flannigan got himself situated in the chair across from me.

"Yeah. We should have. Why?"

"You might have the lab boys compare it to that slug you've got in your pocket."

"Oh? Why?"

"Let's just call it a hunch."

"You've lost me, Frank. That gun you've got in your holster is the one you've always had, isn't it?"

"Yeah. Same old .38 automatic."

"I don't understand. If that gun is the one we have on file, why should we check this slug against it? You didn't fire yours at all, tonight. It sure wasn't the gun that the killer fired."

"I know. Like I said, it's just a hunch, but I think the results might prove—well, interesting."

Flannigan looked at me like he thought I was half crazy. Either that or that I was holding out on him.

"Okay, Frank. What gives? You're sitting there with an expression like the Cheshire cat with indigestion, and you obviously think that there's something special about this slug I've got in my pocket. You've got something on your mind and I think I deserve to know what it is."

"I'm not trying to hold out on you, Flannigan. It's just that I've got this theory, except that it's a little on the wild side."

"So what's this theory?" Flannigan asked. I could tell that I was getting his Irish up again, but I didn't want to let him in on my idea until I was certain. If I was wrong, just the idea would be tough for him to deal with. Of course, if I was right, it would probably be worse.

"I can't tell you. Not now. Not until I'm positive."

"That doesn't cut it, Frank," Flannigan insisted. "I've got two unsolved murders on my hand and we nearly had a third here tonight. I need to know what I'm dealing with. It's pretty clear that you've got some idea of what's going on. Certainly a hell of a lot more than I do. I think it's time you let the cat out of the bag, Frank."

"Look. I told you my theory is wild. If I tell you, you're going to think I'm crazy and you're not going to believe it, anyway. Why don't we just save ourselves both some aggravation and skip it?"

After that outburst, I took a sip of the whiskey. Flannigan glared at me for a second, and then did the same. The rye seemed to calm him down a bit.

"Okay, Frank. No matter how wild this idea of yours is, you obviously have some reason to believe in it. I trust you enough to withhold judgment until I hear you out. I won't think you're crazy. And even if you are, I won't hold it against you. How's that? But I think I need to know what's on your mind."

I could tell that Flannigan wasn't going to let himself be put off. I wasn't sure that I wanted to, any longer either. Part of me wanted to have someone to share my secret with, whatever the implications were for me or that person.

"Are you sure about this, Flannigan?"

"How many times do I have to say so, Frank?"

"Okay. But you've got to promise me that you won't mention a word of this to Janet, or anyone else involved. Not without my say so. Do you agree?"

"Jeez, Frank. What kind of theory is this?" Flannigan exclaimed. "Okay. I promise not to tell anyone."

"This is going to take awhile," I said as I poured a couple of fingers more whiskey in our glasses.

Then I told him. I started off slow, with the time that Janet had walked into my office to hire me to find Handler's killer. After that, I explained how all through the case I kept finding notes that Handler had left for me, notes that detailed the actions that I had just gone through, step by step as if it were all plotted out like one of Handler's mysteries. I ended up with the letter that Handler had sent me, the one he had written the day he had been killed and left with his lawyers to send me when it was all over, the one wherein he claimed that Janet, Armand, Jo, and I had all been created as part of a scheme to bring his murderer to justice. I left out the fact that Flannigan's own name was on the list.

When I was done Flannigan said, "Jesus, Frank. You don't mean to tell me you believe that story, do you? Handler must have been crazy?"

"Maybe he was, Flannigan. But I have those notes. They were all in his handwriting or typed on his typewriter and they all described incidents that happened after he was dead."

"There's got to be some other explanation, Frank," Flannigan protested.

"That's what I thought, too. Or at least that's what I've hoped. Because if it is true—" I didn't spell out what the implications were. I'd lived with them long enough.

"Okay. Let's say that somehow Handler did influence you—"

"Not influence, Flannigan. Create. Let's say Handler *created* me—"

"Okay, created you. I still don't see what that has to do with Black's and Johnson's killer."

"Don't you get it, Flannigan? If Handler *could* create me once to catch his killer, someone else could create another me to do his bidding. Only this new me is like my evil twin."

"Let's just, for the sake of argument, consider for a moment that any of this is even remotely possible," Flannigan said. "According to you, Handler had to go through a whole lot of magical mumbo-jumbo to pull it off. What makes you think anyone else could do the same."

"I don't know. What I do know is that Handler left a notebook. I found it at the bottom of one of these boxes of his stuff. The notebook is a record of all his magical experiments. I think that's what the killer was after tonight."

"Why? Whoever is behind this business already has created his monster."

"Yeah, but maybe he only got half the process right. Or maybe there's some clue to his identity in the notebook. Or maybe a way to uncreate my doppelganger."

"You're what?" Flannigan asked.

"Doppelganger. It's a German term for what I think we're dealing with. The Professor told me about it."

"Great, now we got foreign words to deal with. So this notebook is important?"

"Yeah, or at least the killer thinks so. Or the guy behind him."

Flannigan leaned back in his chair. His hat was pushed back high on his head and he was staring blankly at the ceiling. I couldn't blame him. It was a lot to take in all at once, and most of it was pretty unbelievable. I wasn't sure that I believed most of it myself.

Finally, he took another sip of his whiskey and said, "I'm going to chalk it up to the late hour, or the excitement, or, I don't know, maybe the whiskey. No offense, but this whole story you've spun me is completely crazy. This is real life, Frank, not some god damned fairy tale."

"Look, Flannigan. I don't blame you. I told you it was a crazy idea. I can't say that I believe it all the time, because I don't. Most of the time I just wish it would all go away. But the fact is that there is someone running around out there killing people and he's got my face."

"Yeah, and I'm a policeman, Frank. I'm just a poor, ordinary police detective trying to catch a murderer. Even if half of your story was true, there's nothing in it that will help me do that, so I'm just going to pretend that this whole conversation never happened if it's all the same to you."

"I understand. But now you know why I didn't want to let you in on it."

"I'll say. Let's forget about it. But getting back to the real world for a moment, you said that you recognized the name Frenzel. Who is he?"

"Frenzel?" I asked, happy for the change of subject. "Jerry Frenzel is this writer wannabe. He keeps hanging around anyone vaguely associated with writing mysteries and pushes manuscripts on them trying to get them published."

"I take it they're not so good?"

"They're awful. Worse than awful. Awful can get published if you try hard enough, but his stuff is so badly written that it's not just unpublishable, it's unreadable. I know, he tried to get me to read one of his stories when he found out I wrote *Murder After Midnight*."

"So did this Frenzel ever contact Black or Johnson?"

"Sure. Plenty of times. He's a real pest. I know that he bothered Handler, too, while he was alive. Janet's commented on that a number of times. He was at Sally's wake, too, for that matter."

"Do you think he's capable of murder?"

"Frenzel? The only thing he's capable of murdering is the English language. He's pathetic. He's a forty something loser that lives with his mother."

"You wouldn't happen to know her name, would you, Frank?"

"I don't know. I'm not sure I've ever heard it. No, wait, maybe I have. It might be Ruth."

"Ruth Frenzel? As in the owner of the car your doppelganger drove off in? I think maybe we've finally got a suspect, Frank," Flannigan said triumphantly.

Chapter Eighteen

I offered to pour another couple of fingers of rye into Flannigan's glass, but he said that it was getting late and that he had a busy day ahead of him. I couldn't blame him. It was late, time for all good policemen to be in bed. As for me, well I still had a bit of rye left in my glass and I've never been one to let good whiskey go to waste, or bad, for that matter.

I locked the office door and turned out the overhead light so that the only illumination was that provided by the desk lamp and what leaked in from the street through the front window. Stakeouts tend to be open ended and I'd told Janet not to wait up for me. It was just as well, as I had some hard thinking to do. I poured a little more whiskey into my glass and sat down to stare at the ceiling.

I couldn't pretend any longer. The killer wasn't just some guy in clever makeup wearing knock-offs of my fedora and coat. I'd seen him in the glare of the desk lamp at a distance of maybe a dozen feet. The face I'd been facing had been mine. That had caught me by surprise, which was the reason I hadn't gotten off a shot. There had been a part of me that hadn't been able to shake the feeling that if I had fired, I'd have been shooting at myself. Flannigan hadn't said so, but I knew that his reaction had been the same. The funny thing was, I could have sworn that for just a moment before he had fired, the killer had been going through the same instant of indecision. Maybe that was why he had missed.

But where did that leave me? Who was this guy who could have been my twin? Where had he come from? And why was he going around assassinating mystery writers?

One thing was clear, I wasn't going to come up with answers to those questions staring at the paint peeling off the ceiling. The one place that I might find the answers to those questions was resting in the bottom drawer of my filing cabinet. I hadn't wanted to look there before because I'd been afraid of what I might find, but I couldn't use that as an excuse any longer. The time had come for me to confront my fears and damn the consequences. Somehow, this whole mess was tied back to Ezekial Handler, and the key to unlocking the mystery was in his notebook.

I retrieved the key and unlocked the cabinet. The notebook was still there. There was no reason why it shouldn't have been, but I was starting to view the book as having a life of its own. I picked up the journal, walked back to my desk and laid it out on the desk top. I still had the key to the clasp on my key chain. I inserted it in the lock, turned it, heard the click as the strap came free. This was it, the moment of truth. I took a sip of rye and opened the notebook for the second time.

The first time I had read the book, I had just skimmed through it. This time, I vowed to read it cover to cover. Or at least the parts that I *could* read. Much of the text consisted of arcane alchemical and astrological symbols whose meaning was completely lost on me, as were the passages in Greek and what I assumed was Hebrew. There was a whole page of chicken scratches that I vaguely recognized as Sumerian. There was a lot of Latin, too. I don't read Latin, but some of the words at least were recognizable.

Interspersed with all this gobbledygook, Handler had written comments and notations. I'd missed a lot of them my first pass through, partly because they were located randomly in the rest of the text and partly because Handler's handwriting was quirky and hard to read. This time, though, I was going to make a greater effort not to miss anything.

One paragraph near the beginning caught my eye:

Using various means of divination I have confirmed the gypsy woman's prediction that I am going to die within the year. I have further been able to narrow down the date and determine that my death will be at the hand of Ronald Buckley and will involve an automobile. It would appear, however, that being forewarned does me no good, my death is as inevitable as the motions of the stars. There is nothing that I can do that will alter my fate. The only action available to me is that I may at least obtain justice, albeit posthumously.

The prose was a little flowery for my taste, but the meaning was fairly clear. The paragraph was dated roughly six months before he had died. There was a second date written in the margin, the date of Handler's death. There weren't any details about the "other means of divination," but from the profusion of astrological symbols and mathematical calculations that proceeded the paragraph, I had a good idea of what they involved. Not that I had ever believed in horoscopes or any of that sort of nonsense. Clearly, though, Handler had, though not the kind you read in the papers.

Further along, I found another paragraph, one that seemed disturbingly pertinent to my own existence:

I have decided on the form which my Avenging Angel will take. The old chestnut of wisdom for writers is that you should write about what you know. I've spent most of my life writing yarns featuring hard-boiled private detectives. What better form for my avenger to assume than as a hard-boiled, fedora wearing private eye? A bit of a cliché, perhaps, but then the power inherent in an invocation depends on the prevalence and strength of the archetype on which it is based. What figure has a greater hold on the public imagination than that of the Private Investigator?

One has only to think of Sam Spade, Phillip Marlowe, Lew Archer, even Mike Hammer. I will model him on all those hard drinking, two-fisted, relentless trench-coated heroes that have filled so many of the pages that I have written during my years as an author. I will call him Sam Slade.

The name Sam was crossed out and replaced by Frank. Sam was too derivative, I suppose. Well, there it was, the first expression of my creation, at least if the notebook was to be believed and Handler hadn't been delusional at the time. Reading the paragraph I felt more than a little uncomfortable, almost as if I had been watching my parents at the moment of my conception. That is, if I had ever had parents, which seemed to be in doubt.

On the following pages, there was more in the same vein as Handler elaborated his plan of revenge and justice. Much of it wasn't particularly flattering. I was, it seemed, to be an amalgam of pulp fiction clichés, down to the low-rent office, the rumpled suit, the trench coat and fedora. One thing stuck in my craw, a comment that I need only be "moderately intelligent."

Handler's plan involved not only creating his avenger, but surrounding him with a support network and an environment. Included in the notes were diagrams of the layout of my office, apartment, and other relevant locations. There was also a list of people, Armand, Jo, Flannigan, and of course, Janet. As to why Handler chose to create those four and no others, the notebook offered no explanation.

The next couple of dozen pages were completely indecipherable to me as they were mostly in Latin. The same paragraph was repeated numerous times with minor variations almost as if Handler was trying to perfect the incantation that would bring his plan to life. Then there was this paragraph:

I have made the preparations for my first experiment. Due to the complex nature, I have decided to attempt the creation of the most minor character in the scheme, that of Armand O'Hara, the newsstand operator, in order to perfect the technique for animation. I have obtained the needed supplies and will make the attempt at the next propitious moment.

A list of items in Latin followed. As I said, I don't read Latin, but I recognized the word for blood. There was a description of the steps that were involved in the process and a number of diagrams resembling pentagrams.

As I had discovered the first time I had opened the notebook, the attempt had been a success. At least Handler had discovered that there was a news seller named Armand O'Hara who had been a former jockey until an accident had sidelined him.

After that, there were more pages of charts and symbols leading up to the description of Flannigan. There was also a notation:

That pest Jerry Frenzel interrupted the preparations. How he got in, I don't know. I must have left the door unlocked. I managed to get him out by promising to read one of his wretched manuscripts. I don't think he saw anything of my work. Even if he did, he's too ignorant to understand its nature.

Was Frenzel somehow tied into this business? That seemed unlikely. He'd never struck me as the kind of person that was capable of accomplishing anything requiring real effort.

Reading on, it appeared that the experiment with Flannigan was successful, as was the one with Josephine LaTouche which followed. Jo's role in things had always puzzled me, but then Handler's works had been full of quirky characters which had been part of their appeal.

Maybe Jo had been included in the plot out of force of habit.

There was another comment by Handler, this one more disturbing:

There has been a break-in of the laboratory. Nothing appears to be missing, but some of the apparatus has definitely been moved as has this notebook. I must take steps to secure the house!

The break-in must have upset Handler. He'd never been overly fond of exclamation points. There wasn't any further mention of the incident in the notebook, but I did know from helping Janet deal with the settling of the estate that Handler had had new locks and an alarm system installed about the time of the notation in the notebook.

I had reached the point in the notebook which I had been dreading, the section that involved Janet. The description was far more detailed than that of either Flannigan or Jo. The physical description of her wasn't hard to take. Janet was an attractive woman, as I well knew, though it was disconcerting to have her physical attributes described in the words of another man. It was when Handler went into her relationship with himself that I came close to slamming the notebook shut. It was quite clear from reading Handler's words that Janet wasn't just one of the heroines from his books, but that in her he was creating his ideal fantasy woman, complete with her "undying affection" for the author. I'd hadn't met Janet until after his death, and I'd always known that there had been "something" between them, but to realize that Handler had built in her love for him as part of her creation somehow made me very angry.

Oddly enough, there was nothing in his description of her that dealt with her relationship to me. Was it possible that our love for each other had come naturally and not been foreordained? That, at least, was reassuring.

As with the others, there followed a brief notation indicating the success of the experiment. At least according to the notebook, Handler had succeeded with the creation of Janet Nielsen, who Handler had set up in an apartment, the one where I now lived, as his mistress. Amazingly, by the dates, less than a month had transpired from the first entry in the notebook.

I found the next of Handler's comments interesting:

I have discovered with Janet Nielsen, that once she was created, I am no longer in control of her actions. I had not noticed this with the first three characters, but then I had not made the attempt to get close with them. Janet, however, though she is everything that I had planned for, has begun to act as an independent entity, not necessarily operating in opposition to my plan, but definitely acting in response to her own motivations. I am not sure the effect that this will have on my plans.

Only a dozen or so pages with writing remained—the section that covered my own purported creation. Strangely, I read through these pages with less distress than those relating to Janet. Handler's descriptions of me, while not necessarily flattering, were, I had to admit, accurate; the only thing new was the following comment:

As I have determined that, once created, the characters operate under their own free volition and are no longer subject to my direct control, I must find another method to manipulate Slade's actions so as to effect my goals. I have decided that the best way to do this is to supply him with a sequence of clues that will point him in the proper direction. This is a far less certain method than I had initially intended, but I believe that having created him, I know his mind and personality well enough to predict his actions through the

*first few steps of the plan. Once he has gone that far, I will
have to trust that the clues I have provided and his innate
abilities will be sufficient to steer him to the final moment of
justice.*

This, then, was the explanation of the various messages
that he had left for me to find during my investigation of his
murder. It also explained why the final resolution had not
gone quite as he had planned, even if the goal of bringing
Buckley to justice had succeeded. Only it had been Janet,
and not me, that had been the instrument of his murder's
destruction.

The journal ended with a note of finality:

*It is done. All the characters have been put in place,
including Frank Slade. I have taken what steps I can to
insure the success of my plan, but the final result is in the
hands of whatever powers, if any, control the universe.*

Finis

Ezekial O. Handler

I knew enough Latin to know that the final word meant
"the end."

So that was it. I was no wiser as to whether Handler had
been a magical genius, or just a deluded old man waiting for
the end. Though it was a complete explanation for
everything that had happened, the notebook contained
nothing that could be considered proof that anything
between the covers corresponded to reality.

More importantly, for the business at hand, there was
nothing bearing on the possibility of my doppelganger.
There was no clue as to the identity of such a being and
certainly no mention of a means to combat one. If Handler
had discussed the possibility, he had done so in Latin, and I
was no wiser as to what would happen if I confronted my
evil twin than I had been at the start of the evening.

I shut the notebook, relocking the clasp. As I did so, I noticed that the sky outside my window had turned to the dull gray of dawn.

Chapter Nineteen

That morning, Jerry Frenzel was asked to come down to police headquarters to answer some questions regarding the use of a car registered to his late mother during a break-in the previous night. Unfortunately, the police couldn't do more because Frenzel had earlier reported the car stolen, so technically, there wasn't anything to tie him in to either the break-in or the killer. Flannigan invited me to be present at the questioning. It was an invitation I couldn't refuse.

After being issued a visitor's badge, I was escorted up to the detective's floor where Flannigan was waiting for me. They had Frenzel stashed in one of the interrogation rooms fitted out with one-way glass. Before we went in to talk to Jerry, Flannigan took me in to observe Frenzel. He'd been left to sit by himself for a half hour or so just to see if he'd sweat. An old police dodge, but one that works.

"Doesn't look much like the guy last night, does he?" Flannigan quipped. Seeing as Frenzel was maybe four inches shorter and fifty pounds heavier than either I or my double, it was a pretty accurate comment.

"I never thought it was him," I replied. "But that doesn't mean that he's not behind this business." I hadn't had a chance yet to mention to Flannigan what I'd found in Handler's notebook. I had my doubts as to whether he'd take it seriously, anyway.

"Yeah. Maybe. Well, I think he's had enough time to stew. Let's go see if we can get him to crack."

We went into the interrogation room. Flannigan took the seat across from Frenzel. I grabbed a third chair which had intentionally been placed at the end of the table before Frenzel had been ushered in. Jerry was surprised when he saw me, kind of as if one of his plots had been disrupted, and not entirely pleased about it.

"Hi, Frank," he said quickly, then to Flannigan, "What's he doing here?"

"Mr. Slade has kindly come in to assist the investigation. It was his office that was broken into last night. I'm Lt. Flannigan, by the way. I'm handling this case and several others that we think may be related."

"Oh," Jerry said. "I guess that's okay, then."

"I'm glad you approve. I'm sure you're a busy man, Mr. Frenzel," Flannigan said, knowing full well that Jerry didn't have a job, "so let's get down to business. The burglar was seen leaving the scene of the crime driving a dark green 1966 Ford Fairlane 500 sedan registered to your mother. I understand that your mother is recently deceased?"

"Yes. She passed away six months ago."

"My condolences," Flannigan said. "And you were living with your mother until she died?"

That seemed a sensitive point with Jerry. "We shared a house, if that's what you mean. It was a convenient arrangement for both of us. I could take care of my mother and the house, and it left me the freedom to pursue my writing career."

"I didn't mean to imply otherwise, Mr. Frenzel," Flannigan said in the same flat cop voice he'd used throughout the interview. "I'm just trying to establish some facts. After your mother died, what became of the car?"

"It became mine, I guess. I was an only child and mother left me everything, what there was of it."

"But you didn't change the registration?" Flannigan said, raising his eyebrow just a bit.

"I didn't see any reason too. You see, I don't drive. I never felt the need to get a license."

"But what became of the car?"

"It just sat in the garage." Jerry was starting to get a little agitated. "I'm not sure I see what you are getting at

Lieutenant. As I'm sure you know, I reported the car missing this morning."

"As I said, Mr. Frenzel, I'm just trying to establish the facts in the case. Am I to understand that as far as you know, until the car was stolen, it hadn't been out of the garage of your mother's house since her death?"

"My house now," Jerry said in a huff.

"I stand corrected. Your house. But you haven't answered my question. Had the car remained in the garage?"

"Yes. I'm surprised the thief was able to start it."

"And when was the last time you saw the car?"

"I don't know. Maybe a couple of weeks ago. As I said, I don't drive, so there is no reason for me to go into the garage on a regular basis."

"I see," Flannigan said. "So it's possible that the car may have been stolen anytime in the last few weeks."

"Sure. I guess so," Jerry responded. At least he seemed comfortable with that answer.

"Is the garage attached to the house?"

"No. It's detached, at the back of the lot. It opens out onto an alley. You have to understand that it's an older house."

"Was there any sign of a break-in? A forced entry?"

"No, but then I left the garage unlocked."

"Very unwise of you, Mr. Frenzel. But then I suppose you realize that now."

"It never seemed important," Jerry said defensively. "The car wasn't worth much, and the only other things in the garage were gardening tools and such. Not much for a thief to take."

"Still, it seems that someone did steal your mother's car—"

"My car."

"Yes, your car," Flannigan said. As I sat there watching the exchange I had to smile. Flannigan was working Jerry like a fly fisherman works a trout, putting just the right inflection into his voice to make Jerry nervous without using language that could be construed in any way as prejudicial.

"And at no time during the last several weeks did you hear any suspicious noises coming from the garage?"

"No, but then I've been in and out a lot. Trips to the public library, that sort of thing."

"If you don't mind my asking, Mr. Frenzel, if you don't drive, how did you get around?"

"I take the bus, mostly. Our house—my house, is right on a bus route, so it's very convenient."

"I'm sure. The mayor will be glad that someone appreciates the municipal transit system."

"Is this going to take much longer, lieutenant?" Jerry asked impatiently.

"Not much longer, Mr. Frenzel. I just have a few more questions."

"Very well."

"I believe that you were acquainted with Joshua Black and a Miss Sally Johnson? I understand they were fellow mystery writers."

Jerry started. Flannigan had dropped his bombshell, and gotten results. For a moment Jerry didn't seem to know how to respond to the question. Finally he answered:

"I had met both of them on occasion. On a professional basis. As writers. I can't claim that I was friends with either of them." I had to smile; the last was a great understatement.

"Can the same be said for Ezekial Handler?"

This question really got Jerry flustered. He looked over to me for support. I just stared back blankly.

"I don't see what any of this has to do with a stolen car, lieutenant," Jerry protested. "Just what are you insinuating?"

"I'm not insinuating anything, Mr. Frenzel. It's just that a man matching the description of the man involved in the break-in last night, the man driving your car, was seen at the scenes of both murders. There is the possibility, which we can't ignore, that the man who stole your car is the man responsible for the deaths of both Joshua Black and Sally Johnson. I'm just trying to establish if there are any links between the various crimes. I hope you can understand that, Mr. Frenzel."

"I suppose. Of course, I want to help in any way I can—"

"I'm sure you do, Mr. Frenzel. In that vein, you wouldn't object if I had a forensics team out to examine your garage, would you?"

"Is that really necessary lieutenant?"

"You did report the theft of a motor vehicle, Mr. Frenzel, a vehicle, it turns out, that has been linked to a major crime. I did mention, didn't I, that in the course of the burglary, a shot was fired at a police officer?"

"No, as a matter of fact, you didn't." Jerry was beginning to sweat.

"Obviously, this is a very serious matter. Besides, I'm sure your insurance company will be making inquiries if you should file a claim. The car was insured, wasn't it, Mr. Frenzel?"

"I'm not sure. Mother took care of all those kinds of things."

"I see," Flannigan responded. "Well, if you have no objections, I have a form for you to sign authorizing a search of the garage."

Flannigan slid the form across the table along with a pen. Jerry made a big show of reading it over before finally signing it.

"Thank you, Mr. Frenzel," Flannigan said as he retrieved the paper. "I don't think I have any further questions. Can you think of anything, Frank?"

"No. I think you've covered everything, lieutenant."

"I can go, then?" Jerry said.

"Of course. You've been free to go at any point, Mr. Frenzel. I assure you that you are not a suspect in the break-in, and that your presence here was completely voluntary. Have a nice day."

Jerry got up and left as quickly as he could without seeming to hurry.

After he'd gone I asked Flannigan, "Well, what do you think?"

"I think, Frank, that there was something Mr. Frenzel wasn't telling us. I'm just not sure what."

"So what happens now?"

"I send the lab boys over to Frenzel's garage, not that it will do us much good. Even if we should find the killer's fingerprints in the garage, Frenzel can always say they were left at the time the car was stolen. We still don't have anything to tie Frenzel to the killer."

"What about getting a search warrant for his house?"

"On what grounds, Frank? Having your car stolen doesn't give the police the right to poke around your house. We'll need more than we've got before we go before a judge to get a warrant."

"So that's it?"

"Oh, not quite. I'll send out a couple of detectives to ask the neighbors if they've seen anything suspicious. Like maybe a stranger wearing a fedora and a trench coat. All in the interest of apprehending a car thief, of course."

Chapter Twenty

At dinner that night Janet asked me how the stakeout had gone. It had been after eight in the morning when I'd come in and I'd immediately gone to bed, so we hadn't had any chance to talk.

"It went okay. The guy tried to break into the office, but Flannigan and I were waiting for him. Unfortunately he managed to give us the slip." I didn't see any need to mention that a shot had been fired. Janet tends to get upset about things like that. That's one of the reasons she wanted me to stop being a P.I. "We chased him out of the building, but he had a car waiting and got away. Fortunately, one of the detectives on watch managed to get the license number."

"That was a break. Or was the car stolen?" Janet has read enough crime novels to expect something like that.

"Yeah, or at least that's what the owner says. Funny coincidence though. The car was registered to Jerry Frenzel's mother."

Janet paused, her fork halfway to her mouth. "I thought that she had passed away recently?"

"Yeah, a few months back. Technically, the car belongs to Jerry, only he never got around to changing the title. Seems he doesn't have a driver's license. According to him, the car has been sitting in the garage of his house ever since his mother died. He reported it stolen this morning, but he says he's not sure when it went missing."

"It sounds to me as if you don't believe him," Janet commented.

"I'm not sure what to think. Frenzel never struck me as guy with enough gumption to try anything criminal, but I have to admit, I've gone out of my way to not know the guy."

"That seems to have been the typical reaction." Janet responded. "Jerry is just one of those people who's totally lacking in personal skills. It's kind of sad in a way. Of course that doesn't mean that he wasn't a pest. Zeke couldn't stand him. He actually told Jerry that he'd call the police if he ever caught him at the house."

Handler had lived in an old mansion down close to the lake in the part of town where the beer barons had built their homes back in the last century. It had been a great pile of a place, much too big for Handler's needs, but a great place to write about murder. It wasn't surprising that Handler had ended up spending much of his time at the apartment he had set up for Janet. The mansion had been left to Janet in Handler's will, but she had sold it to a developer as soon as she could. That was just as well, as I couldn't see either of us living in the place.

"Speaking of Handler's place, did he ever mention a break-in there?"

"No, not that I can remember. Why do you bring it up?'

"Oh, no reason, really. It's just that I was going through some of his old notebooks recently, and I came across mention of one."

"He never said anything to me about it. It's not surprising, though. Even when he lived there, half the place was shut up. He only used a bedroom, the parlor, the library and the dining room. Despite the size of the house, he didn't have any live in staff. Just a woman who came in a few times a week to clean. And he spent a lot of nights here for dinner and—"

Handler's relationship to Janet was a subject that we didn't talk about much. There didn't seem much point in dwelling on it, so we didn't.

"Anyway, the place was empty a lot of the time, so it's not that surprising that someone might try to burglarize it."

"But you wouldn't know if he'd ever filed a police report?"

"No. As I said, this is the first that I've heard of a break-in."

"It doesn't matter. I can have Flannigan check to see if a report was ever filed." I tried to sound nonchalant about the whole thing.

"Is it important?" Janet asked. She seems to have a sixth sense about when I am concealing things. Or maybe it's just that she's a woman.

"Frankly, I don't know. There's a possibility that it might be tied into the murders."

"Why would you say that?"

"Well, Handler *was* a mystery writer. Just like Josh and Sally."

"But any break-in there would have to have been a few years ago."

"I know. Like I said, it's probably nothing. Just an irrelevant coincidence."

Janet looked at me like she was trying to get inside my head. "But you think it might have something to do with the murders? And the break-in at your office?"

"It's possible. After all, I've got all of Handler's old manuscripts and notebooks there. Maybe the thief was after something in particular, something that he didn't get the first time. Or maybe it's just that with the city running low on mystery writers, I'm next on the list."

"Don't joke about things like that, Frank." There was a hint of a look in her eye, the look that she'd had when she'd shot Buckley with a .45 Colt. Janet can be very protective at times. It's one her most endearing qualities.

"Look, I'm sorry. I didn't mean to upset you."

That seemed to mollify her and I let the subject drop. We finished the meal with other topics of conversation, but when she'd brought in the coffee and desert Janet asked, "If the person who broke into your office were after something in Zeke's papers what could it be? After all, there are just the notes for his novels and letters between him and his publisher. I suppose some of the original manuscripts for his books might be worth something, but it's not like someone could just sell them. Without provenance, they'd be worthless."

Leave it to Janet to think in those terms. She has a good head for business, amongst other things.

"You're guess is as good as mine."

Later that evening, after Janet went to bed, I stayed up nursing a glass of Scotch. Despite my lack of sleep, I needed to think.

Should I have mentioned the notebook to Janet? Part of me disliked the idea of leaving her in the dark, not only because it's never a good idea to keep secrets from the woman you love, but because Janet is probably a lot smarter than I am, and certainly more level headed. But part of me didn't want to burden her with the knowledge contained in Handler's journal. If the contents were all just some delusion on Handler's part, then there really was no reason for Janet to ever see what was inside. Knowing what was contained in the book could only induce anxiety in her, and I knew from firsthand experience what that could do to a person. It hadn't been pretty. Maybe Janet would handle it better, chances are she would, but did I want to take the chance?

And if Handler hadn't been delusional? I still wasn't sure what that meant. I knew there was a killer on the loose, one with my body, my clothes, my face. He'd killed two people already and he had to be stopped before he could kill again. Somehow, I had a feeling that the person that would stop him would be me. But what would that mean? Would the death of my evil twin somehow result, as the Professor had suggested, in our mutual annihilation, like the collision of particles of matter and anti-matter? I'm no physicist. I didn't have a clue, and nothing that I'd read in Handler's journal had clarified matters. And, if that was the case, would I still have the guts to pull the trigger to put an end to my evil twin? I didn't know the answer to that question, either.

There were other possibilities, as well, and other implications. What if someone else killed my doppelganger? What would have happened if Flannigan had gotten off a shot the other night in my office and killed the other me? Or, if the doppelganger's shot had been a little to the left and gone through my head rather than splitting the difference between me and Flannigan? What would the consequences have been in that case? If I died and my doppelganger survived, would anyone know that he wasn't me? Would he somehow assume my life? Janet?

But the Professor had hinted at even darker possibilities. What if the moment of annihilation resulted not only in the destruction of me and the doppelganger, but everyone and everything that Handler's sorcery had created, Armand, Flannigan, Jo—Janet? Did I dare risk the possibility? Did I dare not to? Did I owe it to the others involved to give them a say in their fates?

I was flying blind and there was no one I could turn to, not even Janet. Especially not Janet. Long after the Scotch was gone I sat there staring into the night.

Chapter Twenty-One

The next day Flannigan called and said he wanted to meet for lunch. I wasn't particularly surprised. He did that sometimes when he wanted to talk over a case unofficially. Though Flannigan was in general liked and respected within the department, he didn't seem to have any close friends that were cops. I guess that being a P.I. or at least a former P.I., I was the next best thing. There seemed to be some unexplained bond between us as well, but I didn't want to go there. Not just then.

He'd picked a gin joint downtown close to headquarters. As the food was good, I didn't mind. It was an old bar that had been a bar since the days when they'd been called saloons. How it had survived during Prohibition, I didn't know. There was probably an interesting story there, but I didn't know it. What I do know is that they don't build them like that anymore; high, painted tin ceilings, shoulder-high wainscoting that had never been painted and showed the scars of a century of drinkers, and a big, carved, dark oak back bar that ran along one side of the long, narrow room.

I had gotten there before Flannigan, so I ordered a beer and commandeered one of the tables along the side opposite the bar so that we'd have someplace private to talk. It was early, yet, but the place tended to fill up quickly with the lunch crowd around noon. Flannigan arrived a few minutes after me.

The sole waitress, a hard looking blonde in her late thirties, came over to take our orders. I ordered a hamburger with Swiss, a raw onion, tomato and lettuce. Janet tries to get me to eat healthy, but sometimes I just have to revert to my old ways. It doesn't seem to matter what I eat, though, I never seem to gain or lose weight. I guess I've just got one of those metabolisms that burns up the fat. It occurred to me that maybe I had Handler to thank for that, that I'd always remain the way he'd described me in his notebook. If that was the case, Handler hadn't been as kind to Flannigan. The lieutenant always seemed to be struggling against an incipient beer belly no matter what he ate or how much he exercised. Flannigan ordered a club sandwich and a tap.

We made small talk while we waited for the food. We'd beaten the mid-day rush, so it didn't take long for our orders to arrive. The burger, when it arrived, was a third of a pound of medium rare beef on an onion roll. It came with a little paper cup of home-made coleslaw and chips. They didn't have a deep-fryer, so fries weren't a choice. Flannigan's club came between slices of lightly toasted pumpernickel, and was dressed with more of the coleslaw instead of mayo. The bar got its baked goods from a German bakery down the street. It was worth it. I ordered another beer to go with the burger. Flannigan said he was fine.

Neither one of us said much while we ate. The sandwiches were good, with nothing of the assembly line about them.

As Flannigan had set up the meeting, I waited to let him start the conversation.

He opened with, "The lab boys gave Frenzel's garage the once over this morning."

"Did they find anything?"

"Not much. The car was gone, of course. No way to say when. Most of the rest of the contents were the usual junk. They didn't have much luck lifting prints off of anything. The place hasn't been painted in years, so the surfaces were pretty well weathered and dirty. Same with the floor, so no footprints."

"Any sign of a forced entry?"

"Hard to say. I talked to the detective that went out with them. He said the place was pretty dilapidated, and that there were probably half a dozen ways that someone could have gotten in without leaving a mark. He did say that there were some marks where the side window might have been jimmied."

"So the guy that took the car got in that way?"

"Maybe," Flannigan replied noncommittally. "I saw photos of the window. The marks were fresh, maybe too fresh, though with it being as cold and dry as it's been the last week or so, it's hard to say when they were made."

"So you think someone, maybe Jerry, jimmied the window to make it look like someone broke in?"

"It's possible." Flannigan shrugged. "For all we know, the marks could have been made yesterday after we interviewed Frenzel. All I know is that the garage had a side door that would have been a lot easier for any self-respecting car thief to have gone in through than climbing in through the window. And just as easy to pry open."

"So Jerry's story about the car being stolen is just so much hot air?"

"Maybe. No way to prove it though. Not that would stand up in court, at least. One other thing, though. The detective I talked to said that Frenzel was acting really nervous—"

"Having a bunch of police technicians going over your property will do that—"

"According to the detective it was more than that. It wasn't the police that he was afraid of, it was something else."

I thought over what Flannigan had said. I couldn't say that I was surprised. Maybe Jerry's car *had* been stolen, or maybe he had leant it to the killer and then tried to cover it up by faking a break-in, which fitted the evidence just as well, but Frenzel was certainly involved in some way. Maybe he'd gotten himself into something deeper than he had planned and was trying to cover his tracks. But if that was case, what was behind it?

"So where does that leave us?" I asked.

"I've detailed a couple of men to keep a watch on your friend Jerry, but I can only do that for a couple of days unless something more solid turns up implicating him. Other than that—I was hoping, maybe, that you'd have some bright ideas."

I took a swig of my beer while I decided how to reply. I wanted to give Flannigan something that would keep him pointed in the right direction. The problem was, that he'd find what I suspected was the truth so fantastic that he'd just ignore it and keep treating the case as a normal homicide. I needed to spin him a yarn that was believable.

"Okay, I've got a theory—"

"Is it has wacky as your last one?"

"It's pretty wild, I admit, but it doesn't involve anything supernatural."

"Okay, shoot," Flannigan said. "At this point, I'm ready to listen to anything."

"Let's suppose that Frenzel gets it in his head that he wants to kill off what he sees as his competition. He can't do it himself; you've seen what kind of guy he is, so he decides to hire himself a hit man. The problem is, being Jerry, he doesn't know any real hit men. But, let's say for the sake of argument, that he does know some out of work actor who looks something like me."

"You and me both saw the killer," Flannigan protested. "He didn't just look a little like you, he was your exact double."

"That's why I say it's an actor. Someone who knows a lot about makeup and imitating someone's mannerisms.

Anyway, Frenzel offers this guy money to bump off Black and Sally Johnson. The only problem is that this guy is an actor, not a professional hit man, so he has to improvise the jobs."

"Okay, what did Frenzel use to pay off the killer? He didn't strike me as being particularly flush with cash."

"His mother died, recently. Maybe she had some insurance. Besides, it might not take a whole lot of cash. Remember, this actor is an amateur, not a pro. He's probably hard up, too. Actors almost always are. He might have been willing to knock off someone for a few thousand dollars. Maybe less. You've known cases where people have been murdered for a lot less, haven't you?"

"Yeah," Flannigan replied. I could see the lights going on inside his head. "I see your point. It makes as much sense as anything. But if it is the case, why is Frenzel afraid? And why did the killer try to break into your office?"

"Let's assume it's like I said, Jerry hires this actor guy to kill a couple of people. Anybody who would agree to that has got to be more than a little bit crazy. Maybe the actor discovers after he knocks off his first victim that he really likes killing people. Maybe he likes it so much that he's no longer doing it for the money. Maybe Frenzel is afraid that *he* might be next. After all, Frenzel is the only person that provides a link back to this actor."

"And what about the break-ins at you office. Why would this actor guy do that? Twice?"

"I don't know. Maybe he was planning on knocking me off? Or he might have been trying to plant evidence. After all, as far as a lot of people know, the killer looks like me. Why not try and make it look like I'm the killer. After all, he doesn't know that I've got a police lieutenant as an alibi for the first murder and a room full of people as witnesses for the second."

Our discussion had been getting pretty heated by this time, so much so that the bartender was giving us suspicious looks. I caught his eye and ordered a couple of more beers.

"I've got to admit, Frank, I thought your first theory was pretty wild, but this one is really out there. You shouldn't waste stuff like that on real life; you should use it in those books you claim you're writing."

"Nah. It's too wild. No one would ever buy a plotline like that in a book."

"You're damned right," Flannigan said.

The waitress brought over the beers. For a moment, Flannigan looked like he was going to turn his down, but then he gave a shrug and took a long pull of his. After he put it down he asked, "Saying for a moment that I believe this theory, what do you expect me to do, check out every actor in the city?"

"Why not? How many can there be? Especially ones that are about my height and weight? And how many of them would Frenzel know? Unless the killer is my long lost twin, he has to know something about makeup. Quite a bit, actually. Who else but an actor or someone else involved with the theater would know that. He might not even be a professional actor, maybe he's someone associated with an amateur group. What's it going to cost you except some extra leg work?"

"So you still think this Frenzel guy is involved somehow?" Flannigan asked.

"Don't you? He certainly acted suspiciously when you interviewed him, and your detective said he acted like he was afraid of something when they checked out the garage. Isn't that enough to at least make him a suspect?"

"Oh, he's a suspect, alright," Flannigan responded, "the question is of what? Okay, I'll have him checked out. See if he knows any actors. Any other suggestions?"

"I'm all out of wild ideas for the moment," I answered.

"I've got to get back to work," Flannigan said. He stood up and finished off his beer. It was only after he'd gone that I realized he'd left me to pay the tab.

The truth was, I didn't believe my little theory about Jerry hiring an actor to kill Josh and Sally. Frenzel's link to the killer was something much darker. I was suspecting, though, that the part of my little story that was true was that Jerry was no longer in control of what he'd created. That was why he was afraid.

When I got back to the office, I checked in with my answering service. I've never liked those machines with the little tapes. When I'd given up the P.I. racket, I'd kept the service. I didn't use it much, but it came in handy sometimes. Of course I sometimes forget to check in with them. In this case it had been a couple of days.

I found out that there were a couple of messages from Max Tully asking me to call back. I called the number he'd left and he answered.

"Frank, I've been trying to get a hold of you for a couple of days now." He sounded upset and a little afraid.

"What's up, Max?"

"Tell me you called me two nights ago?"

"I could, but I didn't." Two nights earlier I had been on the stakeout with Flannigan. "Why?"

"Someone saying he was you called. It sounded just like you. He said he wanted to meet."

"It wasn't me, Max. What did you do?"

"Maybe I'm imagining things. Maybe I'm just spooked by Sally and Josh being killed. Maybe it was what you said about making sure it was you, but something just didn't feel right. I begged off. Said I had a previous engagement."

"You did the right thing, Max. It wasn't me."

"What's going on, Frank?"

"I'm not sure, Max. As close as I can figure, there's some lunatic running around with my face killing people."

"Jeezus, Frank. You're serious, aren't you?"

"Yeah, I'm serious. Two nights ago, this guy took a pot shot at me in my office, so now we know he's 'armed and dangerous.' Don't take any chances, Max."

"So what should I do, Frank?"

"It might not be a bad time to take a vacation. Somewhere out of town."

"You mean it, Frank?"

"It's up to you, Max, but it's not bad advice. Besides, I hear Florida is nice this time of year."

"Hell, it's like I'm inside one of my books."

"Yeah. I've got that feeling, too." Then I got a bright idea. "Max?"

"Yeah?"

"Next time I call I'll say the word 'butterball' so you will know it's me. Got that?"

"Butterball?"

"Sorry, it's the first thing that popped into my head."

"I'll remember, Frank." He hung up.

Chapter Twenty-Two

When I got home that night the apartment the lights were off, which, considering the time of year was unusual. There were no smells of dinner being made coming from the kitchen, either. I turned on the hall light and called out Janet's name. I got no answer. I made a quick circuit of the apartment, turning on the lights in each room, but there was no sign of my wife. In the living room, the drapes were still open, the large windows, black empty rectangles staring into the night. Janet always drew the drapes shut at dark during the winter.

A sudden panic hit me, not that something had happened to her, but that Janet had left me. I'd never quite believed my good fortune in landing Janet, the perfect woman. What had she ever seen in me, a two-bit private eye, who hadn't even been able to handle his biggest case without her help? With her looks and brains, she could have had any man that she had desired, yet she had ended up with me.

In a rush, I went into the bedroom and threw open the doors to her closet. Her clothes were still there, hanging in a neat and orderly row. When I opened the drawers of her dresser, all of her things were still in place. For a moment the scent of her overwhelmed me. I went into the bathroom. Her things were still arranged neatly around the sink, her toothbrush still poised in the stand ready for use. Strangely, it was this latter fact that eased my mind. Janet would never have gone off and left her toothbrush behind, would she?

In less of a panic I checked the hall closet where we kept the suitcases. They were still in place. I went back into the living room and poured myself a drink. After I had done that, I drew the drapes, shutting out the night.

Had I been so preoccupied with the case that I had forgotten Janet mentioning that she had other plans? I didn't think so, but then, would I remember if I had forgotten? It suddenly occurred to me that something might have happened to Janet, an accident perhaps, or an emergency. I checked the pad in the kitchen where we left messages for each other, but nothing had been written down. I placed a hurried call to the answering service, but no new messages had been left.

Janet's address book, the one where she kept the names and phone numbers of her few friends was lying next to the phone, just where she always kept it. I started dialing the numbers, one by one, asking if they knew where Janet might be. No one had talked to her that day or had any idea what plans she might have. Most were solicitous asking if they could help, but a few sounded as if they were thinking, "she's left him at last." It didn't take long to make the calls; there weren't that many names in the book. Neither one of us had a wide circle of friends or a network of connections to the community. Mostly, we just had each other.

Almost as an afterthought, I called the Blue Angel and asked for Jo. Somehow, against all odds, the two of them, Janet, the perfect woman, and Jo, the illusion of one, had formed a bond. I didn't pretend to understand it, but it was real. It took awhile for the bartender who answered the phone to get Jo on the line.

"Frank, darling. What's the matter? The bartender said you sounded desperate."

"Jo, I'm looking for Janet. You haven't seen her, have you?"

"No. We haven't talked for a while. Is something wrong?"

"I don't know. All I know is that when I came home tonight she wasn't there."

"Well, maybe she just lost track of time," Jo replied, trying to sound reassuring. "Maybe she's just out shopping. Us girls do that, you know."

"Not Janet. Not without leaving word. She just wouldn't do that."

Jo was silent for a moment. The thing was, Janet *wouldn't* be late without leaving word. She wasn't that kind of person. She was never irresponsible. She just wasn't made that way. Made that way. The phrase took on a sinister meaning as I thought of Handler.

"Frank? Are you still there?"

"Sorry, Jo. It's just that I'm worried about Janet."

"Of course you are. You don't think that this has something to do with that other business, the murders I mean?"

"I don't know, Jo, but that's what has me concerned."

"Is there anything I can do, Frank?"

"No. Just if you should see Janet, have her call me. Please?"

"Of course, Frank. And don't worry. I'm sure everything will turn out alright."

"Thanks, Jo."

I hung up. Talking to Jo had done me some good. It had slowed my mind down so that I was starting to think rationally. Maybe something had happened, an accident, where Janet couldn't get word to me. The possibility that it might be some sort of ordinary emergency was somehow easier to take. I thought of calling around to the hospitals, but then I had a better idea. Flannigan could manage something like that more efficiently than I could. I called Homicide, hoping that he was still there. He was.

"What is it, Frank? I was just about to go home for the day." Flannigan sounded tired, but then he hadn't been getting much sleep lately.

"It's Janet, Flannigan. She wasn't there when I came home tonight."

"Maybe she's just out with friends or shopping or something, Frank. You know how dames are?"

"This is Janet we're talking about, Flannigan."

"Yeah. Right. What do you want me to do, Frank?"

"I was hoping you could check with all the hospitals, accident reports, that kind of thing."

"Sure thing, Frank. I'll get one of my men right on it. Say, you don't think this has something to do with the Frenzel business, do you?"

"I don't know what to think, Flannigan. All I know is that Janet isn't here, and she's not with any of her friends. She didn't leave a note or anything. I've checked all of that."

"Frank? Was there any sign of a disturbance or a break-in at the apartment?"

"Not that I could see."

"Well, that's good. Where are you now? The apartment?"

"Yeah."

"Okay. Stay there. I'll let you know as soon as we've contacted all of the hospitals."

"Yeah. I'll be right here. And Flannigan? Thanks."

After Flannigan hung up, I started to think about what he had said about a break-in. I got up and looked the apartment over, not as a panicked husband, but as a detective. The front door showed no signs of a forced entry. There was a back door leading off the kitchen that gave access to a service stairs. There was no sign of a break-in there, either, and the deadbolt was locked, as it always was. The apartment was on the tenth floor of a shear-sided building. It had a balcony off of the living room, but it didn't directly abut those of the adjacent apartments. It was hard to imagine someone gaining access, that way. The door to the balcony was always kept locked in any case. Just to make sure, I opened the drapes again and turned on the outside light. A thin layer of snow covered the balcony floor. There were no footprints.

Okay, so there had been no forced entry. Had someone gained access some other way and surprised Janet? I made another pass through all the rooms. My wife was a neat housekeeper, very neat. Nothing had been disturbed.

It occurred to me to check the hall closet. I don't know why I hadn't thought of that before. When I looked, the coat that Janet normally wore in winter was missing. A quick check of the place she usually left her purse showed that that was gone as well. So she had gone out. The questions were when and where?

I called down to the doorman. Yes, it is that kind of building. That was no help as the doorman hadn't been on duty earlier in the day. Could he give me the number of the man who had been? It was important. Something in my tone must have convinced him that I was serious, because he gave me the number. I made the call.

"This is Frank Slade, 10B. Did you happen to notice my wife leaving today?"

"Miss Nielsen? Sure. I got a cab for her. Must have been right before noon. Anything wrong, Mr. Slade?"

"It's just that my wife hasn't come home, yet, and I don't know where she is. You don't happen to know where she was headed, do you?"

"Sorry, Mr. Slade. I just got her the cab."

"But she was alone?"

"Yeah, just her. Anything else I can do for you?"

"No. Thanks, anyway."

So Janet had taken a cab just before noon. That looked like she might be going to meet someone for lunch. But who? And where?

While I was pondering these questions, the phone rang. For a moment, I thought it was Janet, but when I answered it, it was just Flannigan.

"Good news, Frank. The hospitals all checked negative. Same with the accident reports. Even if they didn't get her name a good looking woman like Janet would have been noticed, Frank."

"Yeah, thanks. I think Janet may have gone to meet someone for lunch. Her coat and purse are gone, and the doorman says he got her a cab just before noon."

"Any idea where she went?"

"No."

"I'll make some calls, Frank. Don't worry. We'll find her." We both knew from experience that that wasn't a certainty.

"Yeah. Thanks, Flannigan."

I hung up the phone again, staring at the desk on which it sat. Like everything else in the apartment, it was a neat arrangement of blotter, pen stand, phone, answering machine.

Answering machine!

Why hadn't I thought of it before? I'd never liked the things. They were impersonal and mechanical with their cheap tape recorders, not to mention unreliable. I used a service at my office, but Janet had insisted on having an answering machine at home. I never bothered with it. No one ever called me at home, anyway. But they did call Janet.

I rewound the tape and pushed the "message" button. I'd gone back too far and there were a couple of messages from a few days earlier, one from a store saying that an item had come in for Janet, and another from one of her friends. Then I came to the last one:

"Janet, can you meet me for lunch at Le Bon Frere. There's something important we have to talk about."

The voice on the machine was mine.

Chapter Twenty-Three

I'd been to Le Bon Frere a few times with Janet. It was just the sort of pretentious faux French place that the name implied. The tables were covered in white tablecloths and the place settings had too many forks. The waiters wore short, little jackets and walked around with their noses stuck in the air, which must have made it hard for them to look down them at the patrons. The food was okay, but you couldn't just order a plain steak or a hamburger unless maybe you could do it in French. I doubt if the place even had a deep fryer, let alone used it. Janet liked it.

If what little French I had served me right, the name meant something like "the good brother." In the mind state that I was in, I immediately speculated about the other one, the "bad brother." It didn't matter, though, it was the only clue that I had, so I drove over there. I know that Flannigan had told me to sit tight, but I had a need to do something, anything. If Flannigan's men found something, I could trust him to take care of it. If he didn't, it wouldn't matter.

I found a parking place down the block from the entrance. Inside, there was a balding guy with slicked back hair and the sort of thin moustache one sees in bad movies from the thirties standing behind a podium. I assumed that he was the maitre d'. As I came in the door he took one look at me and decided that he didn't like what he saw. That was okay with me, as I didn't like his looks, either.

"May I help you, monsieur?"

"You can dump the fake accent, Marcel. I happen to know that you were born in Sheboygan." To emphasize the point I accidentally let my jacket slip open to reveal the butt of the .38 automatic underneath. That got his attention.

"What do you want?" He'd slipped the accent. If my guess about Sheboygan wasn't right I'd been pretty close. Like Ashwaubenon, maybe.

"The name is Slade, and I'm a private investigator. I'm here for some information. Give it to me, and I'll get out of your hair, what there is left of it." I flashed my P.I. license in his face to prove I was serious.

"And if I don't?"

"I can have some detectives from the Homicide Squad here in ten minutes, and they can ask you questions the rest of the night."

"Look, I don't need any trouble. What do you want to know?"

"There was a lady, tall, blonde, good looking that met someone here for lunch. Right around noon. I want to know who she met."

"I'm afraid I can't help you. I wasn't here at lunch. I'd didn't come in until five."

"Okay. I assume that with a swell place like this you need to have a reservation. Even for lunch."

"Yes, that is customary."

"So maybe there's a reservation. You could check."

"What name?"

"Slade. Frank Slade." Marcel's eyebrow went up when he heard the name. I couldn't blame him. It must have sounded kind of screwy. I added, "Or maybe Janet Slade."

Marcel pulled out a massive leather bound book from behind his podium and studied it for a moment.

"I'm sorry. There are no reservations under Slade."

"What about Nielsen?"

"No, nothing for Nielsen, either."

I was about to ask Marcel how I could reach whoever had been on duty for lunch when a small guy came out from the back of the restaurant. He was dressed as a civilian, but from his combed back hair I took him for one of the staff. As he walked past us heading for the front door, he gave a double take like he'd seen one of us before. I was pretty sure that it wasn't Marcel that had got his attention.

I called out "Hey, you?"

He turned around and gave a look that asked, "Who? Me?"

"I want to talk to you for a moment."

He looked at Marcel for guidance.

"It's all right, Emile. It seems this gentleman is a private detective. I'm sure that we will all be happier if you cooperate with him. I'm sure that you'll answer any questions. Emile is one of our waiters, Mr. Slade."

"Okay. What do you want?" "Emile" didn't even pretend with the accent. If he'd just got off the boat, it was the ferry from Michigan.

"What I want to know is why you looked surprised when you saw me."

"It's nothing. It's just that I think I've seen you before."

"When was this?"

"Earlier today."

"Tell me about it."

"Well, I was having a smoke outside on the front sidewalk. It was right before the lunch crowd rush, so it must have been just before noon. A cab comes up and drops off this lady like she's coming here for lunch."

"Describe the lady."

"She was a real looker. Tall, blonde, well dressed. A real classy looking dame."

I had to admit that it was a pretty fair description of Janet. "So what happened then?"

The guy looked at me like I was nuts. "Don't you know?"

"Explain it to me."

"You pulled up in a car. An older Ford Fairlane. The woman acted surprised at first. Like she wasn't expecting to see you, but like she knew you pretty well."

"It wasn't me. What happened next?"

"The talked for a few moments and then she got in the car. They drove off together. I went back inside. That's all I know, mister. Honest."

"I believe you. That's all, unless you got something more to tell me."

"No. That's all I know. Say, what gives? You mean that guy with the dame wasn't you?"

"No. That was my twin brother. He's run off with my wife. That's why I'm looking for him. Thanks for your cooperation." I reached into my wallet for a sawbuck and slipped it to the waiter.

The maitre d' looked at me like he was expecting something as well. I gave it to him.

"I appreciate your help. I'll be sure to recommend this joint to all my friends."

Marcel blanched at the thought. "You do that, Mr. Slade."

I left Le Bon Frere then. I'd found out what I'd come for. My evil twin had left the message for Janet to meet her for lunch, and then had been waiting for her when she arrived. A neat little ambush. Janet had had no reason to be suspicious. I'd heard the message on the answering machine. It would have fooled me if I didn't know I hadn't made the call. When the killer pulled up, she probably got in without thinking. By the time she figured out that it wasn't me, it had been too late. That was if she had realized that it wasn't me. Janet had told me that she would be able to tell the difference between us, but I wasn't sure of that anymore.

I spotted a pay phone across the street from where I parked. I dropped a dime in and called Flannigan.

"Frank, I've been trying to reach you."

"Why? Did you find anything?"

"No. I just wanted to make sure you were okay. Where have you been?"

"I found out what happened to Janet. My doppelganger left a message on the answering machine at the apartment for her to meet him at a restaurant. Le Bon Frere. When she got there, he drove up in Frenzel's car and asked her to get in. She did. Then he drove off."

"Where are you now?"

"Just down the street from the restaurant."

"Why don't you go home?" Flannigan suggested. "There's not much that you can do. We can treat this as a kidnapping now. I'll get the word out. Let us take care of it, Frank."

"I can't do that, Flannigan. The killer has got Janet, and I've got to stop him."

"What are you going to do, Frank?"

I answered, "I don't know." Then I hung up.

Chapter Twenty-Four

What was I going to do? I had to do something, I couldn't just leave finding Janet to Flannigan and the police. The problem was that I had plenty of questions but no answers. The only place that I knew that I might find some of those answers was sitting in the bottom drawer of a filing cabinet in my office, so that's where I headed.

Fifteen minutes later I was sitting at my desk, the notebook lay open in front of me lit by the harsh glare of the desk lamp. I'd paged through it a couple of times already, but no revelations had come to me. I couldn't make out half of what was there because it was in Latin or Greek or Hebrew. Even the English parts hadn't shed any light as to where my doppelganger might have taken Janet. I was tempted to seek inspiration in the bottle of rye in the desk drawer, but I didn't. If ever there was a time for clear thinking, this was it.

Time was passing, and I had a feeling that time was one thing I didn't have a lot of. I needed someone who might be able to make sense of the parts of the notebook that I couldn't read. It was possible that someone at the university might be able to do it, but I didn't know anyone there, at least no one that I could go to and say "Some guy that looks just like me has kidnapped my wife, and by the way, I think he was created by one of the spells in this book. Can you give me a hand in translating it?" In any case, did I really want to reveal the contents of the book to someone else? They'd only think me crazy, or worse, they wouldn't.

So where did that leave me? It's not like I knew any experts in dead languages. I just didn't travel in those sorts of circles. So who did I know that might have a chance of helping? Finally I had a question that I could put an answer to. There was one person I knew who might have a chance of helping out. I stuffed the book into a briefcase that Janet had bought me and headed out the door.

I found a place to park that I could get to quick if I had to and then went into the Blue Angel. I figured that I must be like that character in the comics that always goes around with a dark cloud above his head, because the guy on the door took one look at me and just let me by. It was either that, or he had decided that it just wouldn't be worth it to try and stop me.

I'd never been that fond of the Blue Angel, it just wasn't my kind of place, but that night the smoky haze, the peeling paint, and the cheap, garish décor was something familiar, even comforting. If I had been in a different mood, I might have asked what was less of an illusion, the Blue Angel's attempt to recreate pre-war Berlin or the faux French pretensions of Le Bon Frere? But I wasn't in frame of mind for that kind of rumination.

There was a good crowd in the joint that night, most of the tables were occupied and the stools along the bar were full of people waiting for the show to begin. I hadn't noticed before, but the night was still young, less than a couple of hours had passed since I'd come home to find Janet missing.

Jo was chatting up some of the regulars that she knew when she spotted me standing there. She, too, must have sensed the cloud following me around because she made her excuses and came over.

"Frank, darling. What's the matter? You look like your puppy has just been run over."

Jo was looking good. She had on a platinum blonde wig that hung to her shoulders and was wearing a red, floor length gown with plenty of curves built in. If you didn't know better, you might not realize that she was an exironworker. I knew better, but behind the rouge and mascara I saw a friend.

"I've got problems, Jo. Janet's been kidnapped."

"Kidnapped? Oh, you poor boy. Is there anything I can do?" Jo sounded like she was ready to watch my back. I could have done worse.

"I don't think so, Jo. Not right now. What I need is to find the Professor. Do you know if he's in?"

"I haven't seen him yet, Frank, but he might be in his dressing room. You know where that is?" She didn't seem surprised that it was the Professor that I wanted. Longwell has gotten a reputation as a man in the know amongst a certain circle.

"Yeah, thanks, Jo. I know the way."

"Frank, if you need help—" I could see Jo's fists balling up in her opera gloves. I knew she still packed a mean right hook.

I made my way back stage to where the dressing rooms were. On the way I spotted Kenny talking to the bass player. Kenny had on half of the costume he wore for the Professor's magic act. The bass player didn't seem to mind. The two of them looked happy. All I saw was a face I knew.

"Kendra, is the Professor in?" The Professor had told me that Kenny was going by that name, now. Part of the transitioning process, whatever that was. It was none of my business. All I knew was that Kenny or Kendra seemed more confident and happier than when I'd first seen him as a cigarette girl working the front.

"Sure, Frank. He should be in the dressing room."

"Thanks."

I made my way back, found the door and rapped. "It's Frank."

"Come in. I'm decent."

The Professor was sitting at the dressing table, a deck of cards in his hand, practicing manipulating the cards in the complicated one-handed shuffle used by experts in up-close magic. It was something he'd been doing for forty years, and I didn't doubt that he could select which one of the fifty-two cards would come up on top. He took a look at me and set the deck neatly on the table.

"I don't need to be a psychic to know that something is wrong, my boy. What is it?"

"Janet's been kidnapped."

"The doppelganger?"

I just nodded.

"If there is any way that I can be of assistance—"

"I was hoping you'd say that, Professor. I need to figure out where he's taken her. I was hoping that the answer might be in here—" I opened the briefcase and pulled out the notebook. "The problem is I can't read half of what's here. That's where I was hoping you would come in."

The Professor took the book, opened it and began flipping through the pages. As he did so, he was shaking his head.

"Frank, I'm afraid your notions of my abilities far exceed the reality. I'm no scholar. I'm just a two-bit carney and old-school stage magician. My formal education ended when I dropped out of school when I was thirteen and joined the circus. As to my informal education, well, I learned to run three-card Monty with the best of them and all the other cons and scams of the carnival, but this—"

"I've got no one else to turn to, Professor."

"Look, Frank, what Latin I know I got from the nuns in school. I know enough words that I can throw them into my patter well enough to fool the yokels, but that's about it. As for Greek—well I'm afraid it's all Greek to me. I can get by in Yiddish if I have to, but Hebrew? I'm afraid I won't be able to make any more sense of what Handler wrote in this notebook than you can. Probably less."

"What am I going to do, Professor? He's got Janet, and I've got to find her. Who knows what he'll do to her."

"I sympathize, my boy, I really do. If there was any way that I could help you I would."

"If you can't read the book, what about working some of you psychic hoodoo. I know that you see things other people can't."

The Professor shook his head sadly. "You know the gift doesn't work like that, Frank. It's not normally something that I can turn on and off at will. I've got no control over it. Maybe I do see things others don't, maybe I can see auras, but I don't see how that can be of use in this situation."

"What am I going to do?" I repeated. I must have sounded pretty pathetic.

"Don't go to pieces on me, my boy. Now is not the time for that. Save that for later. Even if we can't decipher this notebook, that doesn't mean that you have to give up hope."

"I'm not sure I have any left, Professor."

"Nonsense. You wouldn't be here if you felt that way. If we can't approach your problem one way, then we just have to approach it from another angle."

"I'm not sure I understand what you mean."

"Look, magic might have created this problem, but that doesn't mean it's the only way to solve it. There are other approaches, logic, the process of elimination, deduction. Deduction, that's it, my boy," the Professor suddenly shouted in a burst of enthusiasm

"Deduction, I don't get it."

"But that's just it, Frank. You *do* get it. What are you?"

"What do you mean? I'm a man who's lost his wife, that's what I am."

"No. I mean, *what* are you? You're a detective, that's what you are. If all this business of Handler creating you is real, then what did he create you to be? A *detective,* that's what! From the letter you showed me, Handler claimed that he created you to track down his killer and bring him to justice. That means that he endowed you with all the skills necessary for the task, skills that are exactly the kind of thing that you need to find your wife."

"It was Janet that brought Buckley to justice, not me," I protested.

"But you were the one who tracked him down," the Professor insisted.

"So what am I supposed to do?"

"How should I know? You're the detective. Detect. Find clues. Ask questions. Pound the pavement. Throw out a dragnet."

"You make it sound like this is something out of a book, Professor."

"Well, isn't it? If we accept the proposition that Handler is responsible for you and Janet and the whole business, then it *is* just like something out of one of his books. You are preordained to succeed, just like any other hard-boiled private eye. They may suffer some hard knocks along the way, but they always figure things out in the end."

"Things don't always work out so neatly in the real world, Professor."

"Don't sell yourself short, Frank. I happen to know first-hand that you've had a few success along these lines recently. There was the DuVille case, for one. You found his killers. They were brought to justice. *Ipso facto.*"

"I thought you didn't know any Latin."

"Is that Latin?" the Professor asked with a wink.

"I'll point out that I'd have been a cooked goose in the DuVille case if it hadn't been for Abe Silver."

"That's not the point, by boy. The point is, is that you were the one that put the wheels in motion, that got the ball rolling, that—"

"I get the idea, Professor. This has been a swell pep-talk. But what if this notebook and all the rest of Handler's story is just a bunch of hooey? What if I wasn't created to detect? What if I'm just a two-bit ex-shamus and the guy who kidnapped Janet is just somebody who happens to look like me? What then?"

"That's the beauty of it, my boy. The fact is, you *are* a detective. It doesn't matter if you were created to be one by a spell, or you just became a detective in the normal, mundane course of life. It works out the same, either way. You're a detective, now is the time to go out and act like one!"

Chapter Twenty-Five

I had to admit that the Professor had gotten me all worked up with his little speech. Maybe that was what I had needed. I left the Blue Angel with a new sense of purpose. The question was, what was I going to do about it?

I had to start somewhere, and that somewhere was with Jerry Frenzel. I was certain that Frenzel was the person behind this whole business. Even if he had lost control of his creation, he was the best lead I had as to what had happened to Janet. If I could find Frenzel I could confront him, and even if he wasn't home, I might be able to find out what he'd been up to by searching his home. Flannigan might not have grounds for a warrant, but there was nothing barring a private eye from doing a little breaking and entering if need be.

I drove out to the house that Jerry had shared with his mother before she had died. Like most of the houses on the block, it was a story and a half frame bungalow set on a narrow lot with a postage stamp sized front lawn. It had probably been built in the '20s, and not much had been done to it since. It wasn't exactly dilapidated, but even in the dark I could see that it needed a coat of paint. It either needed to be fixed up or torn down.

I drove past the place, slow enough to check it out, but not so slow as to attract attention. There weren't any lights on. Jerry wasn't home or he was asleep. Either way, in the mood I was in, there wouldn't be anything to stop me from getting inside. At the end of the block, I took a right and parked the car. I checked the .38 automatic in the shoulder holster I wore under my jacket to make sure there was a round in the chamber. From the glove box I got a small but powerful flashlight and a flat little pry bar. If a cop came by I'd have a lot of explaining to do, but I didn't care.

There was an alley running down the middle of the block, a narrow gravel lane with backyard garages, mostly single car, opening into it. It was late enough that none of the houses had lights on, but then it looked like a neighborhood where people went to bed early. From the street I'd counted the number of houses from Jerry's to the corner, so I didn't have any trouble figuring out which was Frenzel's. A rusted chain-link fence ran along the lot line, but there was a gate next to where it ran up to the garage. There wasn't any lock, just a latch which worked quietly enough when I tried it. I opened the gate, went through and closed it behind me without latching it just in case I had to make a hasty exit.

The night was pitch dark, and the garage shielded me from sight as I crept along its side. When I reached the corner, I paused to look around, but there wasn't much to see. The back of the house was maybe twenty feet from me, and I could just make out a small porch and the back door. There didn't seem much point in trying to sneak up on it as there wasn't anyone to see me.

I tried the handle of the back door. It was locked. I risked using the flash to check it out. The pry bar would probably have made quick work of it and I had a set lock picks in my pocket, but on a hunch I lifted up the doormat. Sure enough there was a key underneath it. When I tried it in the lock it worked. As quietly as I could I opened the door and entered.

I was in a small porch that had been enclosed some decades earlier. There was a door leading into the house proper, and when I tried the handle, it proved to be unlocked.

The layout was pretty typical of bungalows of the period. Along one side was the kitchen in the back, a bedroom up front with a bathroom and a set of stairs leading to the second story between them. The other side had a living room in the front and a dining room in the back with a half-wall with some built-in cabinetry separating them. There was no hallway between the two sides and the front door opened directly into the living room. I'd entered through the kitchen.

The house had that peculiar sense of quiet that only an empty house can produce. I decided to risk the lights. They'd be a lot less likely to arouse suspicion than me waving a flashlight around. My guess was that Jerry kept irregular hours. If so, the neighbors wouldn't be surprised to see activity this time of night.

It didn't appear that Jerry was much of a housekeeper. There was a pile of dirty dishes in the sink. I ran my finger over the top one in the stack. The food stains were dried hard. It had been a while since they'd been used which probably meant that Jerry hadn't been home in a day or two. In one way, that was good news. I probably wasn't going to run into Jerry. The down side was that I probably wasn't going to find Janet there, either.

I made my way into the dining room. The furniture was about what you'd expect, some good, some bad, all of it more than a few decades old. There was an open pizza box on the table. It still had an uneaten slice in it, but that didn't necessarily mean that Jerry had been interrupted during dinner. It just meant he wasn't particularly fastidious, but I'd already known that.

The living room was pretty much of a mess, but the kind of mess you get from an aging bachelor, not the kind you get when a place has been tossed. There were piles of books everywhere, mostly detective fiction. There was a desk in the corner with a typewriter. A sheet of paper was sticking out. I gave it the once over. It was another one of Jerry's awful attempts at writing. Nothing else on the desk provided any sort of clue.

I moved on to the bedroom. Unlike the rest of the house, this was still fairly neat though a film of dust was starting to build up. The room must have been Frenzel's mother's. It said something about Jerry that he hadn't taken up occupancy of it though his mother had been dead for months. I looked in the closet, but all I saw were old women's clothes. The same with the chest of drawers. No sign of Janet and no clues as to her whereabouts.

The ground floor had proved a bust. That left me with a choice of up or down. I chose down on the theory that the cellar would be the mostly likely place to keep a captive. It was as good a theory as any, but it didn't pan out. When I checked out the cellar I found just what you would expect. It was a low ceilinged space with exposed joists through which you could see the floorboards above. There was an older washing machine and dryer next to a small sink, a furnace and a tank for the oil that ran it. The rest of the room was full of the normal sort of junk that basements just seem to collect.

I made a half-hearted inspection of the cellar floor looking for signs of a hidden room. I hadn't expected to find any and I didn't. Jerry had never struck me as the handy or industrious type, and it hadn't been long enough since his mother had died for him to do much along those lines, anyway. The floor was cracked in a few places, but it was intact. I headed back upstairs.

I climbed the narrow flight of stairs up to the second floor. That had been divided into two rooms, one in front and one towards the rear with a tiny bathroom squeezed between. It was evident that the front room was Jerry's bedroom. There an unmade bed had been tucked into the front dormer. A set of drawers had been built into the space under the sloping roof to serve as a dresser, with a small closet next to it. It was actually kind of a cozy space, with a ratty but comfortable looking armchair and hassock and a reading lamp along the wall opposite the dresser and closet. An air-conditioner had been set into the window for summers and there was a small space heater for the winters. I felt the space heater, but it was stone cold.

The bathroom didn't have space to hide anything more interesting than a toothbrush. It didn't have a tub, just a sink and toilet. If Jerry bathed, he used the bathroom downstairs.

The room at the rear was set up much like the one in the front except the shed dormer in back provided a little more floor space with headroom. It looked as though Jerry had been using this space as a playroom since he'd been a kid. There were still some toys on the shelves along one wall, including a model train that looked to be thirty years old. More recently, it looked as though it had served more as a workroom. A big table had been pushed up against the dormer window. It was covered with papers and notebooks.

I started poking my way through the mess hoping to find something helpful. Most of what I found were just the sort of notes a writer, even a bad one, keeps; ideas for plots, bits of odd information, notes of works in progress. I had nearly worked my way through the lot when I found it.

"It" was a notebook labeled Ezekial Handler. When I opened it, it was covered with pages of notes about the author, almost as if Jerry had been keeping him under surveillance. From the other stuff I'd gone through, I recognized the handwriting as belonging to Frenzel. I had to say this about Jerry, he might be a slob, but he had beautiful hand-writing, very neat and legible, as if someone had made him practice long hours to perfect it.

The dates in the notebook began about a year before Handler's death, At first the notes were the kind of things that you'd expect from a stalker, time and dates and places of public appearances, details about the author's routine. Then, I came to one curious entry:

I followed Z to an apartment building near the lake. Very swank. Handler had never been there before, I'm sure. At least not in the last six months I've been following him. But he had a key and didn't have to buzz anyone to let him in. I looked at the names next to the buzzers. For some reason, one struck me, "Janet Nielsen." I don't know why, but that name seems to be associated with Z.

It was pretty obvious who "Z" was. Then a few paragraphs later:

I'm sure that before this week there was no such person as Janet Nielsen, but now she seems to be established as Z's mistress. Who is she? Where did she come from? What is Z up to?

I continued to read until I came to this:

Z is obviously up to something. Something BIG. He's been buying up all sorts of old books on magic, and I followed him to this obscure little shop that seems to sell ingredients for magic potions. I'm convinced that Handler is dabbling in magic, real magic, and somehow this has something to do with this Janet Nielsen woman. I must find out, even if it means I have to break into Z's mansion.

There was more along the same lines, with it becoming obvious that Frenzel was becoming obsessed with Handler's interest in sorcery. The notebook ended with an ominous:

I've DONE IT!

There was no explanation as to what "IT" was.

I tried to find more, but if Jerry had kept records, they were someplace else and not in the house. I searched the drawers that had been built-in like in the other room. I didn't find much until I got to the bottom drawer. This held some photographic equipment, a 35mm camera with a telephoto lens, a tripod, things like that. There was also one of those little collapsible "spy" cameras, the ones that use 16mm film and are designed for taking photos of documents. I recognized the type because I had one in my office.

Underneath the camera stuff were a couple of manila envelopes. When I opened the first one, I found that it contained a set of 8x10 prints, mostly of Handler and his house, but also some of Janet, Flannigan, and myself. All seemed to date from around the time Handler had been killed.

The second envelope contained prints that had been made with the spy camera. I recognized what they were photos of. They were from the pages of Handler's notebook. More particularly, they were the pages relating to me. It looked like I now had the link between Frenzel and my doppelganger. Jerry had used the information he'd taken from Handler's notebook to recreate his experiment—and me.

Chapter Twenty-Six

After I had stuffed the photos back in the envelopes, I gave the second floor one more quick once over. There didn't seem to be anything else that might lead me to Janet. It would just be wasting my time to hang around. On a hunch, I picked up the envelopes and made my way downstairs. I turned off all the lights and let myself out through the front door.

Walking back to my car, I thought about my next move. From what I could tell, Frenzel hadn't used the place for his attempts to recreate Handler's experiments, not unless he had done a very thorough job of cleaning up after himself, something that, judging from the state of the place, would seem to have been completely out of character for Jerry. For that matter, there were no signs that the doppelganger had been living in the house. There certainly hadn't been any evidence to indicate that this was where Janet had been brought to after she had been kidnapped. That meant that Frenzel must have another place to work in and for the doppelganger to stay. The question was, where?

Nothing arouses suspicion as much as someone sitting in a parked car late at night, so once I got back to mine I drove off heading in a random direction. I drove around for a few minutes until I found a twenty-four hour drugstore, and parked in the lot. I could sit there while I thought things through without attracting attention.

Turning on the overhead light, I looked over the photos again. The copies of the notebook didn't interest me. After all, the original was sitting on the seat next to me. It was the others, the ones of Janet, myself, and Handler, especially Handler that I studied, searching for a clue as to where Janet might have been taken. There were half a dozen pictures of the mansion that Handler had owned.

Janet had inherited the mansion, but she'd sold it at the first opportunity. It wasn't exactly a cozy place. It had been bought by some developer who had had big plans for it, but as far as I knew, he was still trying to pull the financing for the project together. Meanwhile, the place was just sitting there empty.

"Sitting there empty," I repeated to myself. It was just the sort of place that Jerry Frenzel would look for to conduct his magic. Just the sort of place that would make for a great hideout for a killer. Just the sort of place you might take a kidnap victim to.

The pieces were starting to click into place. Frenzel, in his quest to become a mystery writer, had become obsessed with Handler, obsessed to the point of stalking him. In the process, he'd stumbled across evidence of Handler's magic experiments, even managed to take photos of some of the pages of Handler's notebook, the pages that detailed my creation. It might easily have ended there, except for the death of Jerry's mother. That had made Jerry a free agent. Maybe it had unhinged him, as well. I didn't know or care, I wasn't a psychiatrist. Frenzel had decided to recreate Handler's efforts and ended up with my doppelganger, which he then used to eliminate the competition. He then decides that he needs the original notebook because he had only managed to copy a handful of pages. Maybe he was looking for a way to undo his creation. Maybe just undo me. Somehow, he gets this notion in his head to kidnap Janet. Or maybe that was the idea of my doppelganger. The Professor had said something about losing control. Was Jerry losing control of his monster?

It all fit. It would make a great plot for a novel. Too bad I wrote detective fiction and not fantasy. That didn't matter, though. It pointed me in a direction, the only compass I had at the moment. If my theory was right, I'd find Jerry, my doppelganger, and Janet, all holed up in Handler's mansion.

I went inside the drugstore and found the payphone. I called Flannigan at Homicide, but he was out. The guy that answered wasn't sure where he was or when he'd be back. I left a message saying I'd be at Handler's old place. Flannigan would know the address.

Handler had bought the mansion after he'd had sold his first big book. It was a dark pile of bricks that couldn't quite decide whether it was trying to be Victorian, Georgian, or classical. Some beer baron had built it in the previous century as a place to raise his "kinder." They had probably grown up having nightmares. Now, as I observed it from the street, the few inches of snow that lay on the grounds around it only served to accentuate the dark mass of its masonry. At the best of times it could never have been a cozy place, but on that bleak winter's night, it looked a fitting scene for the climax of a horror show.

I had parked the car in front of the gate leading to the entrance in the hopes that if Flannigan did get my message, he'd spot it and know where I was headed. For what was probably the tenth time that night, I checked the .38 automatic that I carried under my jacket. The flashlight and housebreaking tools were a comforting weight in the pocket of my trench coat. For the second time that night it occurred to me that if a cop were to come along, I'd have some explaining to do. It didn't matter. If Janet wasn't inside, I was out of clues and out of options to try and save her.

There were no signs of life coming from the house, no lights, but it was a big place, and it would be easy enough to hide somewhere in its depths. The front walk hadn't been shoveled and the snow crunched under my feet as I approached the door. There weren't any footprints other than my own, but I knew that the garage was around the rear with access via an alley. That would have been the way Jerry and my double would have brought Janet in.

The front door had been designed to overawe visitors, an eight foot tall portal of iron studded oak looking bleakly medieval. A gargoyle had been carved into the limestone lintel above the door. To complete the mode, a heavy bronze knocker thick with verdigris was positioned prominently in the middle of the door. There was no bell. For a moment, I thought about using the knocker, but instead I reached for the door latch. To my surprise, when I depressed the lever, the latch clicked and the door shifted free. Slowly, I swung it open trying to avoid squeaking the massive hinges.

It was pitch black inside. I pulled the flashlight out of my pocket and turned it on, the narrow beam skittering across the slates of the entryway floor. Shifting the flash to my left hand, I drew my automatic.

I'd only been in the mansion a few times, though I had a general idea of the layout of the ground floor. Before she had sold it, Janet and I had removed all of Handler's papers and personal possessions, but quite a bit of the furniture had been sold along with the house and remained, some of it draped in sheets, but much of it just covered in dust and spider webs.

I paused at the threshold to listen, but all I heard was a bleak silence. Sweeping the beam of the flash across the floor, no footprints disturbed the thick layer of dust. Despite my effort to move silently, my footsteps seemed to echo in the large empty space. It was cold, cold enough that I could see my breath in the beam of the flashlight. The heat had been turned off after Handler's death. Even when he'd lived there, he'd closed up most of the rooms to save money, confining his occupancy to the library, parlor, dining room, kitchen and a bedroom upstairs. I couldn't imagine why he had bothered to live in the house at all, except for the fact that it was a great place to write about murder.

A massive stairway off the entryway led to the upstairs. I thought it unlikely that anyone would be up there. To the left was the parlor, behind that the library with the dining room towards the rear. I knew that Handler had turned the dining room into a sort of laboratory. The chances were good that Jerry would have used the space for the same purpose. When we had cleared out the house, a lot of the magical paraphernalia had been left behind as just so much junk. Neither Janet nor I had cared to deal with it. The library, though, was the more likely place to hole up. Its only windows were on the side of the house and any light in there was less likely to be seen from the street. It also had a good sized fireplace. With the furnace off, that would be the only source of heat.

Each of the rooms to the left had a door off of the hallway that ran from the front to the back, but there were also connecting doors from the parlor through to the library and from the library to the dining room. If Jerry or the doppelganger were around to hear me moving, they'd be less likely to expect me to come in from the side than from the hall.

I opened the door to the parlor and stepped inside, closing the door behind me. There were still a few pieces of furniture in the room, heavy, over-stuffed Victorian divans draped in sheets. I swung the flashlight around the room, but it looked empty. A quick look at the fireplace showed that it hadn't been in use recently. There were no logs in the grate or ashes below.

I started to wonder if my theory had been wrong. Maybe Handler's place wasn't where Jerry and the doppelganger were holed up. Maybe he had found someplace else to work from. I froze for a moment to listen, but the only sound I heard was that of the wind outside.

I started to move towards the door into the library. I had the flash pointed at the door and I was looking in that direction as I maneuvered myself around the furniture. That's why I didn't see what tripped me up.

I caught myself on a settle and pointed the flash at my feet. What had tripped me up was a short, pudgy form on the floor a couple of feet in front of the door. The body—and it was a body, not a living being—was lying face down. There was a small hole in the back and a frozen pool of blood leaking from underneath the body. The wound looked like it had been made by a bullet fired at close range by a medium caliber pistol. Chances were good that it had been made by the twin of the .38 automatic in my hand. I put my finger to the neck to feel for a pulse, but there wasn't any. The body was stone cold. It had been laying there some time, maybe as much as a day. I already had my suspicions, but I rolled the corpse over anyway so that I could see the face. The face was that of Jerry Frenzel.

Chapter Twenty-Seven

It was pretty clear what had happened. Jerry had been shot in the back, probably trying to get away from his creation. Whether the two of them had fallen out or whether the doppelganger had decided he didn't need his creator any more could be sorted out later. But it had been done in cold blood and Jerry hadn't died instantly. No effort had been made to save him. Instead, he'd been left to bleed out on the floor of the parlor.

Frenzel's body told me a couple of things. One was that I had come to the right place. My guess that Jerry had been using Handler's mansion for his experiments in magic had been right on target. The fact that he was dead meant that my evil twin, the doppelganger, had been there as well. But was he still hanging around?

The door into the library was shut. I put my ear to the wood, but I couldn't hear any sounds coming from the other side. If there had been a keyhole, I would have peeped through it in the approved P.I. fashion, but the door didn't have a lock. There was only one thing to do. I placed my hand on the lever of the door handle and slowly twisted.

Easing the door open a crack I tried to peer inside, but except for intermittent flashes of light the room was too dark to make much out. I pushed it a little farther, enough so that my body would pass, and slipped through.

It was a little warmer in the library, at least above freezing. The embers of a dying fire were in the fireplace providing just enough ruddy illumination to make out the shapes of the furniture. The fluorescent tube of a battery powered camping lantern flickered fitfully on a table as if controlled by the hand of a demented telegrapher. It was the flickering that delayed my spotting her.

When I saw her my heart rose in my throat. Janet was in a wooden arm-chair next to the massive table that dominated the middle of the room. She was sitting motionlessly; her head slumped down onto her chest spilling her blonde hair so that it hid her face. As I played the beam of the flashlight over her unresponsive form I could see that she had been tied in place, her arms lashed to the arms of the chair, her feet tied to the legs, and a half-dozen loops of rope wrapped around her body.

I panicked. The woman that I loved, the only woman for me, was sitting bound to a chair in a freezing room in an abandoned house. For all I knew, she was dead. If she was, my life was over. There wasn't anything left for me. That was the way I was made. The last might literally be true, I thought angrily.

I crossed the room to where she sat. She was dressed in a skirt and sweater, but no coat, not nearly enough clothing for the temperature in the room. When I put my fingers on her wrist, the skin was cold to the touch, but I could feel the faint beating of a pulse. I could see that her chest was moving in shallow, arrhythmic breaths. She was alive!

I laid my .38 on the table to have a free hand. Gently, I lifted her chin so I could see into her eyes. Her pupils were dilated into wide black circles. She'd obviously been given some sort of drug to control her. There didn't seem to be any other wound or damage, at least none that I could detect in the light of the flashlight.

I had to get her out of there, get her medical attention. The doppelganger could wait. I put the flash down on the table pointing at her so that I could see and started to work on the ropes. I wished that I had a knife, but I hadn't thought to bring one, and there wasn't a knife or other implement handy that I could spot.

Whoever had tied the ropes had been an amateur, which only made getting her loose all the much harder. There were too many knots in inconvenient places and she had been tied with one continuous length of rope. I had to undo the knots one by one, in the reverse order in which they had been tied, starting at the feet. My fingers were numb from the cold, making my efforts clumsy and slow.

Finally, I got both her feet free and her right arm, the one closest to the table. I was working on her left hand when Janet gave a moan.

I propped up her head again. Her pupils looked more normal. She was still having trouble focusing, but she seemed to be responding to my face.

Gently I slapped her cheeks, trying to stimulate her. "Wake up, baby. Wake up."

Janet tried to say something, but it just came out a moan. I slapped her again.

"Ow."

"Janet baby. Wake up. I've got to get you out of here."

"Frnk. Ish tht ewe?" Her voice was slurred like a drunk's. I thought about slapping her again, but couldn't bring myself to do it.

"Yeah, baby. It's me, Frank. I've come to take you home."

I wished that I had a flask of something on me to try and bring her around, but then it occurred to me that I didn't know if that would be the right thing to do. I didn't know what she'd been drugged with. I didn't know if booze would help or hurt. There were a lot of things I didn't know. Too many. It didn't matter. I didn't have a flask, anyway.

"Frank. Why'd ya tie me up? Ya didn't need t' do that. Ya know that."

"It wasn't me that did it, Janet. It was the other guy. The one that looks like me."

"Jerry did it. He's the one that tied me up. Where's Jerry? I'll give him what for." She was starting to make more sense. There was a hint of outrage in her voice. I took that as a good sign.

"Jerry's not here. He's in the other room." I didn't see the need to mention that he was dead. There'd be time enough for that later.

"Why'd you kidnap me, Frank? I'd have come if you'd asked."

"It wasn't me, baby. Remember. It was the other guy. The one that I told you about. The one that looks like me."

"Oh—sure. I knew that. I knew as soon as I got in the car that it wasn't you. But it was too late then, wasn't it?"

"Yeah, I guess it was. Don't worry, Janet, I'll get you out of here."

"Okay, Frank." She seemed to lose focus then and her head slumped down again.

I tried frantically to get the rope binding her other arm loose. It was taking forever. She was shivering and I could hear her teeth chattering. I thought about covering her with my coat, but that would have hampered my efforts at getting her loose.

Janet roused herself again. "Why'd you make Jerry tie me up for, Frank?"

"It wasn't me, it was the other guy, remember. The one that looks just like me."

"You never tol' me you had a twin, Frank."

"I didn't know I had one. Besides, we're not really brothers."

"How's he your twin, then, Frank?"

"It's complicated, Janet. I'll explain later. Once I get you away from here."

"What's his name?" she insisted.

"Who?"

"Your twin, that's who?" The drug was still making her loopy. She was thinking and talking like someone coming off a three day bender.

"I don't know. Frank, I think."

That seemed to puzzle her. "Isn't that confusing?"

"Yeah. One of me is enough."

"That's what I always thought, Frank. One of me and one of you."

I would have kissed her right then and there if I hadn't been busy.

"That's right, Janet. Just the two of us. Keep thinking that way. I'll have you home in no time."

That seemed to make her happy. Her eyes were focusing better, and she was staring at the ropes holding her left arm to the chair.

"What's going on here, Frank? Why am I tied to a chair?" It was almost as if a switch had been thrown in her brain. Suddenly she was speaking with her normal clarity.

"You were kidnapped. By Jerry Frenzel and some guy that looks just like me. They lured you into a car and drugged you."

"This is Zeke's old place, isn't it?"

"Yeah. Jerry and his buddy have been using it as a hideout."

"When I get a hold of that little weasel—"

I still didn't see any point in telling her that Jerry was lying dead in the next room.

Suddenly, the pieces seemed to fall into place for her. "The guy that looks like you—he's the one that killed Josh and Sally, isn't he?"

"Yeah. I'm pretty sure. The thing is, he might still be lurking around here somewhere. That's why I've got to get you out of here."

"But you've come to rescue me, haven't you, Frank? My knight in shining armor." I couldn't tell if she was going loopy from the drugs again or not, but it made me feel good.

"Yeah. I've come to rescue you."

I went back to working on the ropes. I had the ones on her left arm almost undone. I was so busy at it that I wasn't paying attention. Suddenly, I heard a gasp from Janet.

"It's about time we met, Frank. Don't you think so?"

I turned around. There I was standing in the doorway to the dining room, dressed in a trench coat and fedora in the best approved private eye fashion. I was holding a .38 automatic in my left hand. Except it wasn't me. It was the doppelganger.

I looked at Janet. Her head had slumped back down onto her chest. I couldn't tell if she was faking it or not. I saw my automatic where I'd laid it on the table. My doppelganger saw it too.

"Why don't you step away from the table, Frank? We wouldn't want anything to happen to Janet, would we?"

"No, we wouldn't." I stepped away from the table, my hands raised. The black hole in the tip of the .38 following my movements.

"That's good, Frank. Just remember, I'm the one with the gun."

"I'll keep that in mind."

"We've got a lot to talk about, you know. Jerry wasn't very good at explaining things. There's a lot that we need to have explained, isn't there?"

"Yes, I imagine we do." I couldn't quite figure out what the doppelganger's game was. Was he just wasting time, or was he really trying to find out how he'd come to be.

"So why don't you start."

"Me? I would have thought it would work the other way around. But I'm okay with that. What do you want to know—Say, what do I call you, anyway?"

"Why, you can call me Frank. Frank Slade."

Chapter Twenty-Eight

"I take it you were the one that killed Frenzel?"

"Who else? It certainly wasn't our girl friend, there." The pistol in his left hand pointed in her direction for a second before returning to me. The way he said it was curious, as if Janet couldn't kill someone just because she was a woman. It showed he didn't know a thing about women—or Janet. The man facing me wasn't me; he didn't have my memories or my life, only my face.

"Why? After all, he created you, didn't he?"

"That's what he said, but that was just a load of bull. You don't expect me to believe a story like that, do you? But to answer your question, I shot him because he was a loser. That and the fact that he was annoying me."

It's quite a thing, to look into your face and see a psychopath staring back at you from your eyes, but that was what I was facing. Somehow, when Frenzel had worked his spell, something had gone missing. My doppelganger had been created without any moral compass. Why had I turned out different? Was it because Janet had grounded me in some way? I didn't know the answer to that question, but I had a feeling it was going to be important.

"I never particularly cared for Jerry, myself, but I never shot him, either."

"Yeah, well maybe you and me are different despite the face."

"Fair enough. Let me ask you this, If Frenzel didn't create you, how do you explain your lack of memories? I assume that you don't really remember anything before you woke up here a few weeks ago."

"So what if I don't? There must be some sort of explanation. Amnesia? Maybe I was in an accident or something? Maybe it was drugs? That Frenzel guy had been doing all sorts of weird things. Maybe he gave me some drug to wipe out my memories?"

I seemed to have struck a nerve. The doppelganger was getting defensive. Maybe the way to get out of this situation I was in was to talk my way out of it. For the moment, I didn't seem to have any other options.

"I suppose that's possible," I said, trying to sound skeptical. "Only I've never heard of any such drug. Not one that worked so completely."

"Are you a doctor, Frank? I thought you were just a two-bit private eye."

"I gave that up. I'm a writer, now."

"And I'm the guy standing here with the gun. Don't forget that, Frank." He said my name with an ironic inflection, as if questioning my right to it. I found it annoying.

"Oh, trust me, I won't."

"Good. So if I'm the guy with the gun, why are you the one asking all the questions?"

"You were the one that said we needed to talk," I replied. I knew I was playing a delicate game, trying to keep the doppelganger off balance without pushing him over the edge, but I didn't have much choice. "If you've got questions, go right ahead and ask them."

"No. You seem to be doing alright at that. Keep them coming."

"Okay. If that's what you want, Frank. How about, why'd you killed Joshua Black and Sally Johnson? What were they to you?"

"That was all Jerry's idea. I wasn't sure what the setup was around here, so I just did what he told me. Actually, killing them wasn't Jerry's idea. He just wanted me to go talk to Black pretending to be you. I was supposed to convince him to help get one of Jerry's books published.

The problem was, Black figured out that something was wrong. I guess I panicked, so I picked up that dingus and hit him over the head with it."

So Jerry hadn't been such a bad guy, after all, just an incompetent bungler. I still didn't feel sorry for him though, not after he'd created this mess Janet and I were in.

"And Sally? She was just a nice old lady who liked to play poker and have a drink. Why'd you killer her, too."

"Same deal. I went to her place just to talk to her about Jerry's book. I think she caught on to me, too. But then I saw the knife. Well, you know what happened next."

"Yeah," I said. There was a sour taste in my mouth. Two people that I had liked had died, and it hadn't even been intentional.

"Let's leave that aside for the moment. Why'd you try to burgle my office?"

"That was Jerry's idea, again. He said you had a notebook that he needed. Something that this Handler guy had kept."

"Did he say why he wanted it?"

"No. He didn't say, but after I killed the old lady, I think he was maybe having second thoughts about me, like he didn't trust me anymore."

I nodded in the direction of the other room where Frenzel's body lay. "Looks like maybe he had a reason."

The doppelganger gave a little chuckle at that. "Yeah, maybe he did, at that."

"Now we get to the big question, Frank. Why did you kidnap Janet? What was that suppose to achieve?"

"Don't you get it, Frank?"

"No, I'm afraid I don't, Frank. Why don't you explain it to me?"

"I may as well. In the end it won't make any difference."

I was wondering how long I could keep him talking, that and how long it would take Flannigan to get my message and come to the rescue.

"Still—I'd be interested."

"I'm sure you would, Frank. It's pretty obvious, isn't it, that there's one too many Frank Slades in this world. One of us has to be eliminated, and seeing as I'm the one with the gun, we both know who that's going to be."

"Okay. Let's say you kill me. How are you going to convince people that you are me?"

"That's where Janet comes in. I take over your life and I take over your wife. With her vouching for me, who's going to argue about it? Besides, she can help me with all the little things, the details about you that I don't know. I figure that in a few weeks, no one will be able to tell the difference."

"And me? What happens to me?"

"Again, that should be obvious. The police are looking for a killer that looks just like you, Frank. I'll supply them with a body."

He seemed pretty confident about his plan. I didn't have the heart to tell him that our fingerprints didn't match, at least not in a way that would fool the police.

"And Janet's just going to go along with this scheme?"

"What choice will she have? Besides, what difference does it make, you or me. We're both alike, aren't we?"

The thing was he was right, in a way. Physically, looking at him was like looking in a mirror, but there was more than that. Looking at him, talking with him, I could see aspects of my own personality, not all of which I liked. One thing that we shared though, was a sense of doubt about ourselves, if only I could play on that.

"How do you explain that away, by the way? That the two of us are identical?"

"I don't know. I guess I haven't thought about it much."

"But you should. You're counting on the fact that you can get away with impersonating me. But why is that, Frank? We don't just look alike. We're identical."

"So maybe we're twins. Identical twins. Separated at birth. Like in the stories."

"I'm not so sure that's going to fly. I don't remember having a twin. Do you?"

"No. But then I don't remember anything from more than the last few weeks. Do you?"

"Well, no. I don't remember much from before the moment that Janet walked into my office and asked me to find Handler's killer. Why do you think that is, Frank? Why can't we remember?"

"Amnesia. Or like I said, drugs."

"Both of us, Frank? Isn't that a bit too much to be a coincidence?"

"I see what you're playing at, Frank. You're trying to confuse me."

"No, this is important. To both of us. Why don't we have a past? Is it maybe because we really don't have one? That we really were created? A product of a spell? Me by Handler, and you by Jerry?"

"That's talking crazy, Frank. Magic isn't real. Everybody knows that. You're just trying to distract me. You're hoping I'll drop my guard so that you can get the gun away from me and shoot me, so that you're the only one of us alive. If I'm dead, than you don't have to worry about someone taking over your life. But, remember Frank, that works both ways. I ought to shoot you now and get it over with. I can convince Janet later. When she wakes up, I'll be the one alive. She won't have any choice then but to accept me as the real Frank Slade."

His voice was verging on the hysterical. I'd pushed him pretty close to the edge, maybe too close. I had to string him along a little longer and hope that Flannigan would get here in time.

"I wouldn't do that, if I were you, Frank."

"Do what?"

"Kill me."

"Why shouldn't I? It would certainly simplify things, wouldn't it?"

"How much do you know about this business? About how we came to exist?"

"What do you mean?"

"Did Jerry explain it to you?"

"No. He just said that he made me and that I had to do what he said. I guess I showed him, didn't I?"

"Yeah, you sure did. But didn't he ever mention the implications?"

"The implications? What implications?"

"Think about it a minute, Frank. We're not just two guys that happen to look like each others. We're not even identical twins. We're two identical copies of the same person. And that's something that's not supposed to happen. It's not natural. Because of that, there's a down side."

"A down side? What do you mean? You're just trying to confuse me."

"No, I'm not. I'm trying to explain things. Because this is important, Frank. Like I said, we're not just twins. We're linked. We're bound together. And there's a good chance that whatever happens to one of us will happen to the other."

"What do you mean?"

"Look, I don't know all the details, but I was talking to a guy I know, the Professor. He's real smart about stuff like this. He said that you're what is called a *doppelganger*. He said that the two of us are bound together by something he called a quantum entanglement. I'm not sure what that means, exactly, but the upshot of it is that whatever happens to one of us is going to happen to the other. So if you go ahead and shoot me, you'll just end up killing yourself."

"That's a lot of nonsense, Frank. You're just trying to talk me out of shooting you."

"Sure. Why not? Whether it's true or not, I'll be dead either way. The question is, will you be dead, too?"

"Don't think you can out-smart me, Frank. Remember, our brains are the same."

"That's just what I've been saying, Frank. We're the same. Not two people, but one, spread across two bodies. There are consequences when that sort of thing happens."

"What kind of consequences?"

"The Professor said that there are all sorts of stories and legends about what happens when a doppelganger and the original confront each other. The outcome is never pretty."

"Those are just stories, fiction. You should know all about fiction, Frank."

"Yeah. Maybe they are just stories. But why would they persist through the centuries and across cultures if there wasn't some truth to them?"

"I don't know and frankly I don't care, Frank. Don't think you're going to talk me out of shooting you."

"I'm not worried about myself. I figure that I'm a dead man whether the stories are true or not. I'm just worried about collateral damage."

"Collateral damage?"

"Do you know about matter and anti-matter, Frank?"

"Anti-matter?"

"Yeah, anti-matter. And this is physics, Frank, not folklore. When a particle and its anti-particle meet, they destroy each other and release a lot of energy in the process. The Professor thinks that you and me might be like that, me the particle and you the anti-particle, and if we react, there will be a huge amount of energy produced as a by-product. Enough to take out this house, maybe the whole city. Do you want that to happen?"

"Shut-up, Frank. I'm done talking, and so are you. If I'm going to end up destroyed, I don't care what happens to anyone else."

I guess that was what was different between me and the doppelganger. I did care. I cared about Janet, I cared about Flannigan, I cared about Jo, and Armand, and the Professor and Kenny and every other person in the world. I didn't know if any of what the Professor had said was true. He had admitted that he didn't really know, either. I just didn't want to take the chance, but I sensed that I'd pushed my double just a bit too far.

I risked a glance over at Janet. She was still bound to the chair by her left arm, but the rest of her limbs were free. If I could distract the doppelganger, she might be able to get clear. But was she conscious? Her head was hanging down, but her eyes weren't closed. One of them winked at me.

I could see that the muscles in the doppelganger's hand were getting ready to pull the trigger. That's when I heard Flannigan's voice calling my name from the hallway.

The doppelganger turned towards the sound, the pistol following his gaze.

I called out "Flannigan, in here."

The doppelganger turned back towards me just as the door between the library and the hall opened.

Then the roar of two shots being fired echoed through the room.

Chapter Twenty-Nine

It occurred to me that I wasn't dead. A bullet from the doppelganger's automatic hadn't pierced my breast or split my skull. Nor had the doppelganger and I dissolved in a primordial implosion. It appeared that the Professor's fears on that score were unfounded.

In the seconds after I realized this, I looked around the room. Janet was still bound to the chair by her left arm, but with her right she had picked up my .38 from where I had placed it on the table and fired at the doppelganger, hitting him between the eyes. The service revolver in Flannigan's hand must have fired at nearly the same instant, his bullet striking the target in the back of the skull. The doppelganger had never had a chance to fire, and the body had now slumped to the floor. The two bullets, Janet's and Flannigan's, arriving nearly simultaneously, had done terrible damage to the head of my double.

After a moment's paralysis I rushed to Janet's side and hurried to untie her left arm. As soon as she was free I took her in my arms. She returned the embrace, my pistol still gripped in her right hand.

"Are you alright, Janet?"

"I'm fine, Frank. I'm the one with the gun, remember."

"Yeah." I planted a big kiss on her mug.

We might have said more, but Flannigan chose that moment to cough to get our attention.

"I take it this is your double, the one that killed Black and Johnson? It's kind of hard to tell now, except that he's wearing a trench coat."

Flannigan was right. The face of the body on the floor was unrecognizable as even being a face. As for the body, well it was about my size, but so are a lot of guys.

Flannigan continued, "I only got a look for a second as I came in the door. I saw he was about to shoot, so I shot first."

"How could you be sure it wasn't me?"

"Fifty-fifty chance," Flannigan said with a shrug, then added, "I saw that he was holding his gun in his left hand. Besides, I didn't think you'd shoot an unarmed man. What does it matter? I was right, wasn't I? Wasn't I—?"

"Yeah. You got the right one. What took you so long to get here? I had a devil of a time keeping the killer's attention long enough for you to show up."

"Is this the gratitude I get? I didn't get the message until I called in. Then I had to find the address of Handler's old place."

"Well you got here just in time. Thirty seconds later and I'd have been the one laying on the floor. Speaking of which, Jerry Frenzel's body is in the next room."

"Were you the one that shot him?" Flannigan asked, suddenly sounding like a cop again.

"No. I'm pretty sure our friend on the floor did it. Maybe as much as a day ago. The body is stone cold."

Flannigan went through to the other room to check. It didn't take him long. He was back in a few seconds. "I'll let the coroner sort things out. And the D.A., though it looks like it's mostly over except for the paper work."

Flannigan sent one of the officers that had come in with him back to the car to radio it in.

"I know it's been a long night for you two, but I'm going to have to file a report. Mind if I ask some questions?"

"No, go ahead. But do you mind if I throw another log on the fire. It's cold in here."

I didn't wait for his permission. While I was at it, I found Janet's coat and draped it over her shoulders.

After that, Flannigan got out his notebook and pencil and got statements from both Janet and I. Janet's story was pretty much as I'd figured it out. She'd gotten into the doppelganger's car thinking it was me, only to find out it wasn't once it was too late. He'd put something over her mouth, probably a rag with chloroform, and the next thing she remembered was my trying to bring her around by slapping her face.

"What made you think of this place, Frank?" Flannigan asked when we were done.

"It was just a hunch. I tried to think like Frenzel. He knew this place was empty and that it would make a great hideout. Really, I didn't have any other ideas, so I came here after trying to call you. The door was unlocked when I got here, so I let myself in. I nearly tripped over Jerry in the parlor. I found Janet and was trying to untie her when the killer came in. After he got the drop on me, I just tried to keep him talking hoping you'd show up. And like I said, you got here just in time."

"Yeah. Glad it worked out that way."

"Me too."

After that the crime scene team arrived to take their pictures and measurements. There were more questions. One of the other detectives took down formal statements for Janet and me to sign. It was nearly four before we got out of there.

On the drive home I asked her, "How much of what I said to the killer did you hear?"

"Not a lot," Janet admitted. "I was still pretty fuzzy from the drugs. What I did hear didn't seem to make a lot of sense."

"It was mostly just stuff that the Professor had fed me one afternoon in the office. I wasn't trying to make sense, just keep him occupied."

"As I said, I don't remember much of it."

I let it rest at that. I couldn't tell if Janet was lying or not. She probably suspected a lot more than she was letting on to.

I drove home and put Janet to bed.

In the morning, she was her normal self. She made bacon and eggs for breakfast. We didn't talk much about what had happened.

The case was a sensation in the press for a few days and then something else occurred and everyone forgot about it except those of us that had to pick up the pieces.

The body of the killer was never identified. The fingerprints didn't match any of those in the state or F.B.I. files, which considering everything isn't surprising. Not much was made of that, because lots of people aren't in the files. He also didn't match any missing persons cases, either locally or nationally. The fact that the face was so messed up pretty much excluded trying to identify him that way. All the official documents ended up reading "John Doe." They couldn't very well have read "Frank Slade." That would have raised too many questions.

It was never sorted out which bullet ended up killing him either, Janet's or Flannigan's, but then, no one put too much effort into making the determination. The dead man was a killer and a kidnapper; both shooters had acted to prevent "imminent danger" to another person, namely myself. The press were about evenly divided as to which was the hero, though Janet's picture, being far more attractive, was the one that made the front pages and TV. My part in the whole thing was pretty much ignored, which was fine by me.

When the *post mortem* was done on "John Doe" the cause of death was pretty obvious. There wasn't enough left of the face for anyone to note the remarkable likeness to yours truly, which is just as well. The only curious finding of the autopsy was the discovery that all the internal organs had been flipped left to right. The condition was considered anomalous, but certainly not unheard of in medical history. No unusual conclusions were drawn from it. The fact never ended up in the papers.

Flannigan stopped asking questions about the time the D.A. did, which was just as well, as I didn't have any answers for him.

Life gradually returned to normal. About a month later *Death Buys a Condo* was released with modest but encouraging sales for a second mystery novel. Josh Black's last book stayed on the top-seller list for six months, and Sally Johnson's novels enjoyed a brief but deserved revival. It was a shame that neither one of them were around to see it.

Though his part in the business never went public, the Professor and Kendra played a month long stint in Las Vegas, and I think they'll be back working the Catskills this summer. Jo is still singing at the Blue Angel.

Life goes on.

Epilog

I'm sitting in my office. Outside, fat, fluffy flakes of snow are falling that, for a few hours at least, will cover the dirt and grime of the city's streets. I should be working, but instead I'm sitting here thinking, trying to make sense of the whole business.

I should be working on a new novel. I've set aside *Bloody Mary, Mob Hit-Woman* to work on it. It's about an unsuccessful writer who meets an out of work actor at a group therapy session. The actor just happens to look a lot like one of the writer's competitors, who is the real hero of the novel. Both the actor and the writer are a little unhinged, and they cook up this plot for the actor to kill off all the other writers in town disguised as the hero. The writer thinks it's all just a joke, but the actor takes it seriously and starts killing people. The hero becomes the chief suspect, and has to solve the case to clear his name. It's a crazy idea, but my publisher loved the idea when I pitched it to her. She said that given my association with the Black and Johnson case it could be a big seller. Me, I'm just hoping that people will think it's what really happened.

I should be working on the book now while the story is still hot, but instead I'm sitting here thinking. There are a lot of unanswered questions. That seems to be the story of my life, literally. A lot of questions and no real answers. And in the end, I'm the only one still asking.

In a way, it's a good thing that the bullets that tore through the killer's head made such a mess of his face. It saved a lot of awkward questions from being asked. Like, why did he look so much like me? As it is, the only people who ever really got a good up close look at the killer that are still alive are Janet, Jo, Flannigan, and myself, and I can count on the fact that none of them will make any waves.

As far as everyone else is concerned, the killer may have born a superficial resemblance to me, accentuated by dressing himself up in a trench coat and fedora similar to the ones that I wore, but that's all. Lots of people look like lots of other people, so it's no big deal.

Officially, at least, it was an open and shut case. There was plenty of physical evidence in the form of fingerprints and ballistics to tie the doppelganger to the murders of Jerry Frenzel, Joshua Black and Sally Johnson and the break-ins at my office. Along with Janet's story about being kidnapped and her subsequent rescue, it made what is called "a compelling narrative." The D. A. was satisfied and so was the press, and that's what matters, isn't it.

But that still leaves a bunch of questions on the table, ones that like I said, I'm the only one asking.

The Professor dropped by the other day and we tried to hash things out over half a bottle of rye. The Professor's the only one besides me who has a real hint of the full story. I could tell that he'd been thinking about it a lot. Some of his ideas were pretty far out there, but I'm not sure I've got any better.

Question 1: Why did my doppelganger end up playing Mr. Hyde to my Dr. Jekyll? The Professor had plenty of speculations on that one. The simplest explanation was that Jerry had been as bad of a magician as he had been a writer. That's the one that I prefer. It's also possible, that because he'd only been able to photograph part of Handler's notebook, some critical part of the spell had been left out. One of the Professor's ideas was that it was all quantum mechanical, something to do with the Pauli Exclusion Principle, and the fact that no two particles can occupy the same energy state. I didn't understand half of what he was saying and thought the other half was pretty far-fetched.

Question 2: Why didn't the doppelganger and I just go poof when he was killed? The Professor admitted that the whole idea of the two of us being linked and suffering the same fate was more of a literary convention than an actual part of the theory. Not exactly something he had made, but close to it. He claimed that he'd never been sure of that part and was glad that things had worked out the way they did. So am I, I guess.

Question 3: Had the killer really thought that he was me, or at least my doppelganger, or had he just been some accomplice of Frenzel's that had pretended to be me?

Question 4: The BIG QUESTION. Had any of this whole doppelganger business been real? Or, had Jerry Frenzel, having run into someone who looked a lot like me, and having read parts of Handler's notebook, come up with a crazy scheme to convince this person to impersonate me. Had Jerry really gone off the deep end and actually started to believe that he had created my double and somehow convinced his accomplice of the same thing? Had Handler really found a way to bring fictional characters to life, or had he been as delusional as Frenzel?

I'd been over that ground before, and I'd never arrived at a satisfactory answer. The evidence, as they say, was inconclusive. I'd concluded long ago that it was better not to ask the question, but this whole business had brought all the old doubts back to the surface.

In the end, neither the Professor and I had come up with any answers we could be certain of. It looked like we never would, even if we finished the bottle of rye, so we called it quits.

I've never mentioned any of this, anything about Handler's notebook or his final letter, to Janet. I feel bad about keeping secrets from her, but there's no reason she has to know. It could only cause her needless anxiety. I think she knows that I'm not telling her everything, but she knows that I'm trying to protect her, too. She's okay with that. Not happy, necessarily, but okay with it. As I've mentioned, she's the perfect wife.

When the dust had settled, Flannigan let me into Frenzel's place so that I could gather up anything relating to me or Janet or Handler. With a closed case, the D.A. didn't care. I said that I was doing it to avoid bad publicity. He was okay with that. He knows there is more to it than that, but he's also learned not to ask questions when you might not be happy with the answers.

I burned all of Jerry's papers. I cleaned up anything that was at Handler's mansion, as well. I debated about what to do with the notebook, but in the end, I tossed it onto the flames as well. The world isn't ready for that kind of thing yet. I doubt if it ever will be.

So I'm left in that old familiar place, not sure about what's real and what's not. Was Handler really a wizard? Am I one of his creations, a character brought to life out of his imagination? Or was it all a big delusion on his part, a delusion that I got dragged into, whether by accident or design?

I don't have an answer. I probably never will, especially if I stop asking the question. If only I could. So I'm sitting here in a dingy office as the snow falls softly outside covering the grime and the dirt and the secrets.

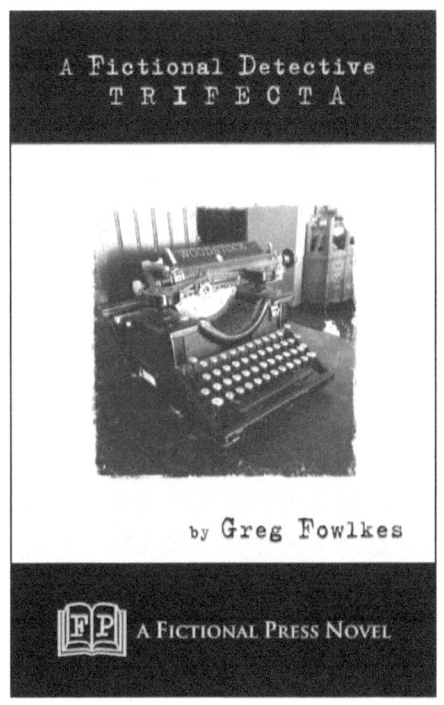

A FICTIONAL DETECTIVE TRIFECTA:

THE FICTIONAL DETECTIVE SPEAKS WITH THE DEAD

BY GREG FOWLKES

A Fictional Detective Trifecta:

The Fictional Detective Speaks with the Dead

My name is Frank Slade. I'm a private detective. At least I think I am. Oh, I'm sure I'm a private dick, but some things about my last case have caused me to question my reality. I'm a man without a past. Before a few months ago there's nothing to prove I ever existed, no paper trail, no public record. My own memories from that time are all kind of vague and hazy. And generic, like they were details created by someone making them up. Like maybe someone named Ezekial O. Handler, the mystery writer that got bumped off not too long ago by his publisher. Oh, there are a few people who claim to have known me, like Flannigan, a police detective, but when I checked into it, his past is no more substantial than my own. Handler wrote me a letter in which he claimed he was responsible, that he had created me to avenge his death by means of some spell he had gotten out of an old book, just like he had created Flannigan, Armand the ex-jockey who operates a newsstand downstairs, a female impersonator named Josephine LaTouche, and Janet Nielsen, my fiancée and Handler's old girl friend. It was a pretty wild claim, even if it did seem to fit the evidence. But Handler had proved to have a good idea of the events that followed his death. If I were a thinking man, it might have bothered me, wondering whether I was real or not, but I'm just a simple private gumshoe and the whole thing is just too existential to worry about.

The current reality is that I'm a private detective with an office in a low rent building in a not particularly nice part of town. The office is what you'd expect would come out of the imagination of a mystery writer known more for his lurid titles than his high literary style. Of course, it's also just the sort of office a not terribly successful P.I. might rent. There's the frosted glass in the door with my name in peeling black paint, the second hand furniture, the bottle of bourbon stashed in the desk drawer. It's the kind of office that you've seen at the start of a dozen mystery movies and read about in more pulp thrillers than you can count. I won't describe it in detail, you can visualize it perfectly without really trying.

Like I said, I'm a private dick, though my fiancée is trying to get me to quit. It's too dangerous she says, and after Handler left her the rights to his last book, the one published after he was killed, it's not like we're going to need the money. She says I should try my hand at writing, detective fiction stuff, says I'd be a natural at it, and with the Handler connection I'd have no problem finding a publisher. What the heck. I might as well give it a try, so here goes. This is an account of my most recent case as it actually happened. It might even be real.

I was sitting in my office going through my files. This was a couple of weeks after I'd solved the Handler murder. That case had left me with a lot of unanswered questions about the nature of reality and I'd gone into a kind of funk that ended up in a week-long drunk. After I'd sobered up I came to the conclusion that no matter what the truth was, there was nothing I could do about it and I might as well just get on with life. After all, it wasn't shaping up as such a bad life. Janet and I were talking about getting married. Janet is the kind of dame men dream about; tall, good looking with curves in all the right places. She was smart and had money, too. We'd be fixed for life with what Handler had left her in his will.

I was thinking about getting out of the business, and was trying to tie up loose ends. I wasn't really looking for any new cases, but I was still listed in the phone book and business directory and it still said "Private Detective" under my name on the frosted glass in the office door. I wasn't completely surprised then, when there came a tentative knock on that door. It was a woman's knock, quick, light, not so much demanding attention as imploring for it.

I stood up, stashed the bottle of bourbon and the glass in the bottom drawer and went to open the door. The last time I had done that, the woman had been Janet, a leggy blonde with looks straight out of a fashion magazine. My visitor was nothing like that.

She was a big woman, not fat, but ample, probably in her mid fifties. She was dressed expensively in a dress and coat that actually fit her and made her seem thinner than she really was. Her hair had been styled recently in one of those cuts that women who can afford it wear. She reminded me as much as anything of the heavy set broad who always played the older rich dame in the Marx brothers movies. You know the one I mean, the one who never seemed to get the jokes.

"Mr. Slade?" she asked tentatively.

"That's me. What can I do for you?"

"I believe you are a—a private detective?"

"That's what it says on the door, though I'm thinking of getting out of the racket."

"Oh—I'm sorry. I thought—" I could see she had trouble on her mind. I never could turn down a dame in trouble, even an older one.

"Please, come in. The least I can do is hear your story. After all, you came all this way down here to talk to me."

"That's very kind, Mr. Slade." She entered the office and took the chair facing the desk. Despite her size she moved with a certain kind of grace. I shut the office door and sat in my desk chair.

When I was seated she said, "I don't quite know where to start."

"Why don't we start with the simple things. Like your name."

"Yes. Of course. I'm Geraldine DuVille. My husband was Herbert DuVille. He ran a trucking business, Tri-State Transportation Services, until he died recently."

"My condolences, Mrs. DuVille. Just what did you want to consult with me about?"

"Well, it's like this, Mr. Slade. Some time before his death, my husband took on some partners. He needed some capital to expand the business."

"How was the business doing, if you don't mind my asking?"

"Quite well, I think. I never bothered too much about the business. I left that to Herbert. But we had always lived quite comfortably. Herbert was a good provider." I could hear the love in her voice. "I'm not sure why Herbert felt the need to expand, but he seemed to think it was important."

"And these partners he brought on? Were they on the up and up?"

"They seemed to be at first. They were just going to invest some money and leave the running of the business to my husband. But after awhile they wanted to become more involved. He never said anything about it, but I could tell that Herbert wasn't altogether happy with the situation."

"Any particulars?"

"As I said, Mr. Slade, I never involved myself with the business. And then Herbert died, and that changed everything."

"Just how did he die?"

"An accident, or so I thought—"

"But something has caused you to change your mind?"

"I'm getting to that. The arrangement as I understand it was that my husband retained fifty-one percent of the company while Mr. McClure and Mr. Trentino split the remainder of the shares between them. However, there appears to have been an unfortunate clause placed in the contract by which they invested. In the event of the death of any of the partners, their share of the company would be split between the surviving partners. The result was that when my husband died his share of the company went to Mr. McClure and Mr. Trentino, and I was left with nothing."

"Your husband didn't leave anything to you?"

"Oh, no, Mr. Slade. I don't want you to think that. He left me the house, of course and some investments. There was also a large insurance policy that he had taken out shortly after we were married. I don't want you to think that he left me a pauper. I may not be able to live quite as well as before, but I shall get by. But it's the thought of the company that Herbert worked so hard to build just going to those— others that bothers me."

"You've talked to a lawyer about this, haven't you?"

"Yes. He said that it was an unusual agreement, but it seemed perfectly legal. He didn't hold out much hope for litigation, I'm afraid."

"I'm sorry about your troubles, Mrs. DuVille, but I'm not quite sure what it is you want me to do?"

"What I want you to do, Mr. Slade is come to a séance."

"A séance?" I said with surprise. It was about the last thing I had expected.

"Yes, a séance, Mr. Slade. I know that this may sound to you like a strange request, but I have been in touch with my husband, and he wishes to speak with you personally. There is something that he wants to tell you."

"You've talked to your husband? At a séance?"

"Yes."

"And he asked for me?" I couldn't keep the skepticism out of my voice.

"Yes. He was quite particular about that point. At the last session he asked for you. That's why I came down here, Mr. Slade. I assure you that I don't normally employ private detectives."

"I didn't think you did, Mrs. DuVille. I admit that I have very little experience with these kind of things, but isn't this an awfully specific request for someone who is dead to communicate."

"I assure you, Mr. Slade, that this séance was not a silly parlor game like those Ouija boards. The Professor is a very serious person."

"The professor?"

"Yes, the medium. Professor Longwell. He's quite well known, Mr. Slade."

"I'm sure he is." Probably by half the bunko squads in the state, I thought to myself.

"I detect a note of doubt, Mr. Slade, but I am willing to pay you for your time, whatever your standard rate is. Please, won't you come? I'm a desperate woman." She seemed on the point of tears.

"It's a hundred dollars a day. Plus expenses."

"What's a hundred dollars?"

"That's my standard fee, Mrs. DuVille. When is this séance?"

"Tonight, if you can make it. I'm sure I can arrange it with the Professor. He's been so helpful."

"I'm sure he has. As it is, I am available tonight. What time?"

"Would nine o'clock be possible?"

"That shouldn't be a problem." Janet was going to fix me dinner, but we'd be done in plenty of time.

"Fine. Here's the address," she handed me a card with her name and address.

"Tonight, then. And don't worry, you can pay me after the séance."

"Thank you, Mr. Slade. I'll be waiting for you."

She rose and I escorted her to the door.

After she left, I thought about the deal. Was she just some poor widow being preyed upon by a charlatan? Or was there more to this séance business? I didn't really believe in ghosts. On the other hand, I didn't not believe in them either. I'd seen enough strange things lately to keep an open mind. Of anyone in the world, I was the last to question the reality of such things. Or the reality of anything, for that matter.

I remembered reading about Herbert DuVille's death in the papers, but couldn't recall any of the details. It hadn't made much of a splash, just a few column inches in the financial section. The death had been ruled an accident. A jewelry heist the next day that had left two dead had pretty much seized my attention along with that of just about everyone else in town.

I decided to give my favorite flat-foot a call. He worked the homicide squad, and if there was anything about DuVille's death that hadn't made the papers, he'd be the one to know.

The phone rang three or four times before a voice announced, "Homicide, Lt. Flannigan." He didn't sound happy. Like he wasn't getting enough sleep.

"It's Frank. Got a minute?"

"Oh, sure, Frank. I've got plenty of time for cheap private dicks. After all, that's what we're here for, isn't it?"

"I can sense that you're busy, so I'll make it quick. What do you know about Herbert DuVille's death?"

"DuVille? It was ruled an accident. Some boxes fell on him at his warehouse or something like that. Why the interest?"

"His widow was just in my office. Apparently her husband has something he wants to tell me."

"Her husband, huh? Wait a minute. Is this some kind of gag, Slade? Her husband's dead."

"It's no gag, Flannigan. Or if it is, it's on me. She wants me to attend a séance. She claims her husband is going to communicate with me from beyond."

"Beyond what?"

"You got me."

"You're not taking this seriously, are you Frank?"

"I don't know. Like I said, his widow was in my office wanting to hire me. She seemed kind of upset. The way I figure, it's probably some huckster trying to take advantage of a poor widow that just happens to have some money. I thought I'd go to this séance and maybe find the hidden wires or whatever."

Flannigan said, "I thought you were thinking about getting out of the P.I. business, Frank."

"Yeah, I am. Janet doesn't like the idea of me putting myself in danger. But how much risk can there be at a séance?"

"I don't know, Frank. Some of these older dames can get some crazy ideas."

"I think I can protect myself. By the way, you wouldn't know anything about a Professor Longwell, would you?"

"Who's that?"

"He's the guy that's holding the séance. The medium."

"Not my line, Frank, but I can ask the guys in Bunko if they've ever heard of him."

"That would be swell, Flannigan. I'll be at Janet's until about 8:30."

"A hot dame like that, and you want to run around messing with ghosts. If you ask me, you're the crazy one, Frank."

"I get that a lot. Let me know if you find out anything. I'll let you get back to your corpses, Flannigan."

I found myself talking to a dead phone. Flannigan had cause for being short of patience. He had been putting in long hours working the jewelry heist murders. A salesclerk and the store's owner had been found dead. Over a million in prime ice was missing, too, without much in the way of clues.

I looked at the clock on the wall. It was getting late, and Janet was expecting me for dinner. I didn't want to disappoint her.

The Fictional Trifecta is available now on Amazon!

Sneak Preview

The Uncorrupted Corpse

A new Greg Fowlkes novel
Now Available

THE UNCORRUPTED CORPSE

EPILOG

They exhumed Vlad Romanescu's body today. The court order listed the reason as the need to get DNA evidence to close a couple of murder cases in Columbus, Ohio. Most of us who were involved in the case though, just wanted to reassure ourselves that he was still there. Not that there was any rational reason to believe his body wouldn't still be in the grave, but the case had affected everyone it had touched. No matter what they *believed*, there were still doubts lingering in the dark corners of their mind.

That's why we were all there on that cold, rainy morning as they dug up the casket, Hazeltine, Murphy, the Smercheks—and myself. The Smercheks had come separately. Vern Smerchek had called me a few months earlier, just to talk I think. He hadn't been drinking. He told me that he and his wife Ellen had separated. That happens sometimes after a child dies. He said he wasn't sure if they'd get back together. I hadn't told him what I thought would happen.

Usually exhumations don't draw many people. Just the cemetery staff and the driver of the medical examiner's meat wagon, and maybe someone from the D.A.'s office if that's where the exhumation request originated. Maybe a family member or two. There was a regular crowd for this one. No family members of course. We never did find any family for Romanescu. Naturally the D.A. himself was there along with a prosecutor from Ohio. It had been a big case, thirteen bodies, not counting Romanescu. As I mentioned, Murphy was there. He had been the homicide detective working the case. Besides the Smercheks there were friends and families of some of the other victims. A couple of reporters and a crew from one of the TV station were in attendance as well.

And me. I had met many of them, but didn't say hello except to give a curt nod to Murphy. It wasn't that kind of occasion. We all just stood around grim faced as the back-hoe removed the dirt over the grave.

Finally they were done with the digging. A sling was suspended from the scoop of the back-hoe so that they could raise the casket from the hole. The workers did their thing and the coffin was lifted up and set on the grass next to the opening. It was dead quiet in that way that happens when there's a drizzle and a thick fog sets in. All you could hear was the clank of the workers' tools as they opened the casket and the sound of crows perched in the gray enshrouded trees in the distance.

They finally got the casket open. Normally they would just put the body on a Gurney and hustle it away in the meat wagon as quickly as possible. The D.A. was smart though. He knew that there were people who wanted to see for themselves that the body was still there. People that needed to see. He knew, because he was one of them. So, before they moved the body, he let people file by the open box to look. They weren't gawking, they were making sure.

I took my turn after Murphy and before Hazeltine. I'd never thought Romanescu had looked all that great before he was killed. They hadn't embalmed him. Something about a clause in his will. Still, he looked about the same after six months in the ground as he had walking around.

Except for the hole in the middle of his forehead where Murphy had shot him with a .38 caliber round. That and the stump of a pool cue that was still sticking out of his chest. That had been my contribution to the affair. I was glad that they hadn't removed it. Not that I believe in those kind of things. Hazeltine had strongly suggest decapitating him and placing the head in the casket face down, but the D.A. had nixed the idea as going too far. That would be an admission of something no one wanted to think about.

Everybody had their look and then the D.A. gave a nod to the M.E.'s man to take the body away. People began moving off to their cars. No one was talking. The grim expressions hadn't left their faces, either, but they looked a little more reassured now that they had seen that the body was still there. Murphy, Hazeltine and I adjourned to a bar for the drink we all felt the need for.

From the Wizard at Law Series by Greg Fowlkes

The Laws of Magic

Egil Njalsson was an aspiring lawyer. A lawyer with a difference. Not only had he passed the bar, but he had an undergraduate degree from the most prestigious school of magic in the country, the California Institute of Thaumaturgy. Needless to say his caseload and clients tended to the unusual. Like witches; or vampires. And the opposition, well they were likely to be demons. But Egil Njalsson had sworn an oath to uphold the law of the land, and... *The Laws of Magic*!

Trial By Magic

Egil Njalsson is just another practicing attorney. Except, that is, for the occasional unusual client. Such as the ghost who retained his services using e-mail. Or the wolf who has been cursed by an Indian shaman to turn into a human during the full moon. Or the Leprechaun who is facing the loss of his saloon. Even when the clients are human, they have unusual problems like the Creole chef accused of making a rival a zombie or the scientist accused of transmuting a man into a statue of silicon. Yet somehow, Egil manages to resolve all his client's problems whether legal or magical. Of course it helps that he is a wizard as well as a lawyer.

Trial by Magic includes five new tales from the same world as *The Laws of Magic*.

FROM THE MURDER ON MARS SERIES BY GREG FOWLKES

BLOOD REDS SANDS OF MARS

On Mars the wind was rising. The grains of sand could be heard abrading the thin aluminum skin that was the only protection against the outside. On the far side of Olympus Mons a prospector lies dead in the sand. Inspector Erik McKernan, head of the handful of men that make up the small Martian police force must find the killer while threading the maze of corporate and international politics that govern the planet, and he must do it while trying to survive . . .The Blood Red Sands of Mars!

A DEATH AT STATION ALPHA

Station Alpha, a remote Martian research facility isolated by a planet wide dust storm. When one of the scientists is found murdered, it falls to Inspector McKernan to determine which of the remaining twelve people at the station wielded the fatal weapon. But, as the crime was committed in a locked laboratory with no possible access and all the suspects would seem to have unbreakable alibis, it will take all his skills as a detective to solve the puzzle of A Death at Station Alpha. Thirty years in the making, the long awaited sequel to The Blood Red Sands of Mars.

A Corpse in Hut Town

Hut Town is the remnants of the original Martian settlement; a collection of inflatable buildings abandoned by the Trust Authority and the mining corporations and now occupied by those catering to the baser needs of miners and construction workers in for a spree. But when a corpse is found in one of the service tunnels, Chief Inspector McKernan is called in.

He has plenty of questions. Who's body is it? How did they die? How did they get to Mars in the first place, and why weren't they missed? And the most important one on the Inspector's mind— are there any more bodies down there?

Murder at the Mars Club

The Mars Club was the sanctuary of the rich and powerful on Mars, so when one of the members is found dead, Chief Inspector is called in to solve the case as discretely as possible. Will the solution of the case prove to be the one man he'd least like to implicate?

FROM THE FICTIONAL DETECTIVE SERIES BY GREG FOWLKES

THE FICTIONAL DETECTIVE

Mystery writer Ezekial O. Handler has been killed in a suspicious car crash. Private detective Frank Slade has been hired by Handler's beautiful girlfriend to investigate. Handler, seemingly with a premonition of his death, has left a trail of clues. Can Slade discover the murderer, or will he instead uncover a secret that will shake his existence to the core?

A FICTIONAL DETECTIVE TRIFECTA

The Fictional Detective has gotten out of the Private Investigator game. Instead, he's trying to write hard-boiled masterpieces such as *Death Buys a Condo*. But despite the fact that the door of his office now says WRITER, some of his clients haven't gotten the word. And a strange lot of clients they are. A man that only contacts him during séances because, well, he's dead; a female impersonator who has inherited a house that's just a little too haunted for the market, and a small time gambler who's trying to end an affair with Lady Luck.

Three All New Novellas featuring the Fictional Detective!

SPACE OPERA NOIR!

STAR CITY STORIES: SPACE OPERA NOIR
FEATURING FRANK SLADEK
BY GREG FOWLKES

The mean streets of Star City, a hollowed out asteroid circling a failed star in the middle of nowhere breed a special sort of man. With grifters, hoodlums, and two-bit con-men from every planet In human space trying to make the big score, it takes someone like Frank Sladek, sometime private detective, sometime finder of lost items, to navigate the maze of corruption and double-crosses that is Star City. As quick with his wit as with a needler or laser pistol, Sladek can handle anyone, except maybe the dames. These are just a few of the Star City Stories.

BOOKS BY GREG FOWLKES

From the Wizard at Law Series:
The Laws of Magic
Trial by Magic

From the Murder on Mars Series:
Blood Red Sands of Mars
A Death at Station Alpha
A Corpse in Hut Town
Murder at the Mars Club

From the Fictional Detective Series:
The Fictional Detective
A Fictional Detective Trifecta

Star City Stories: Space Opera Noir Featuring Frank Sladek

The Uncorrupted Corpse

Tequila Visions

Cargo From Paradise

Ice Viking

The Fictional Press
www.TheFictionalPress.com

The Fictional Press is an imprint of Intrepid Ink, LLC. Find out more at www.TheFictionalPress.com.

About Intrepid Ink, LLC

Intrepid Ink, LLC provides full publishing services to authors of fiction and non-fiction books, eBooks and websites. From editing to formatting, from publishing to marketing, Intrepid Ink gets your creative works into the hands of the people who want to read them. Find out more at www.IntrepidInk.com.